WOLFBANE

WOLFBANE

FREDERIK POHL AND
C. M. KORNBLUTH

WILDSIDE PRESS

Originally published in *Galaxy Science Fiction*,
October and November 1957.

Published by Wildside Press LLC.
www.wildsidebooks.com

CHAPTER I

Roget Germyn, banker, of Wheeling, West Virginia, a Citizen, woke gently from a Citizen's dreamless sleep. It was the third-hour-rising time, the time proper to a day of exceptional opportunity to appreciate.

Citizen Germyn dressed himself in the clothes proper for the appreciation of great works—such as viewing the Empire State ruins against storm clouds from a small boat, or walking in silent single file across the remaining course of the Golden Gate Bridge. Or as today—one hoped—witnessing the Re-creation of the Sun.

Germyn with difficulty retained a Citizen's necessary calm. One was tempted to meditate on improper things: Would the Sun be re-created? What if it were not?

He put his mind to his dress. First of all, he put on an old and storied bracelet, a veritable identity bracelet of heavy silver links and a plate which was inscribed:

PFC JOE HARTMANN
Korea
1953

His fellow jewelry-appreciators would have envied him that bracelet— if they had been capable of such an emotion as envy. No other ID bracelet as much as two hundred and fifty years old was known to exist in Wheeling.

His finest shirt and pair of light pants went next to his skin, and over them he wore a loose parka whose seams had been carefully weakened. When the Sun was re-created, every five years or so, it was the custom to remove the parka gravely and rend it with the prescribed graceful gestures...but not so drastically that it could not be stitched together again. Hence the weakened seams.

This was, he counted, the forty-first day on which he and all of Wheeling had do-nned the appropriate Sun Re-creation clothing. It was the forty-first day on which the Sun—no longer white, no longer blazing yellow, no longer even bright red—had risen and displayed a color that was darker maroon and always darker.

* * * *

It had, thought Citizen Germyn, never grown so dark and so cold in all of his life. Perhaps it was an occasion for special viewing. For surely it would never come again, this opportunity to see the old Sun so near to death....

One hoped.

Gravely, Citizen Germyn completed his dressing, thinking only of the act of dressing itself. It was by no means his specialty, but he considered, when it was done, that he had done it well, in the traditional flowing gestures, with no flailing, at all times balanced lightly on the ball of the foot. It was all the more perfectly consummated because no one saw it but himself.

He woke his wife gently, by placing the palm of his hand on her forehead as she lay neatly, in the prescribed fashion, on the Woman's Third of the bed.

The warmth of his hand gradually penetrated the layers of sleep. Her eyes demurely opened.

"Citizeness Germyn," he greeted her, making the assurance-of-identity sign with his left hand.

"Citizen Germyn," she said, with the assurance-of-identity inclination of the head which was prescribed when the hands are covered.

He retired to his tiny study.

It was the time appropriate to meditation on the properties of Connectivity. Citizen Germyn was skilled in meditation, even for a banker; it was a grace in which he had schooled himself since earliest childhood.

Citizen Germyn, his young face composed, his slim body erect as he sat but in no way tense or straining, successfully blanked out, one after another, all of the external sounds and sights and feelings that interfered with proper meditation. His mind was very nearly vacant except of one central problem: Connectivity.

Over his head and behind, out of sight, the cold air of the room seemed to thicken and form a—call it a blob; a blob of air.

There was a name for those blobs of air. They had been seen before. They were a known fact of existence in Wheeling and in all the world. They came. They hovered. And they went away—sometimes not alone. If someone had been in the room with Citizen Germyn to look at it, he would have seen a distortion, a twisting of what was behind the blob, like flawed glass, a lens, like an eye. And they were called Eye.

Germyn meditated.

The blob of air grew and slowly moved. A vagrant current that spun out from it caught a fragment of paper and whirled it to the floor. Germyn stirred. The blob retreated.

Germyn, all unaware, disciplined his thoughts to disregard the interruption, to return to the central problem of Connectivity. The blob hovered....

From the other room, his wife's small, thrice-repeated throat-clearing signaled to him that she was dressed. Germyn got up to go to her, his mind returning to the world; and the overhead Eye spun relentlessly, and disappeared.

* * * *

Some miles east of Wheeling, Glenn Tropile—of a class which found it wisest to give itself no special name, and which had devoted much time and thought to shaking the unwelcome name it had been given—awoke on the couch of his apartment.

He sat up, shivering. It was cold. The damned Sun was still bloody dark outside the window and the apartment was soggy and chilled.

He had kicked off the blankets in his sleep. *Why couldn't* he learn to sleep quietly, like anybody else? Lacking a robe, he clutched the blankets around him, got up and walked to the unglassed window.

It was not unusual for Glenn Tropile to wake up on his couch. This happened because Gala Tropile had a temper, was inclined to exile him from her bed after a quarrel, and—the operative factor—he knew he always had the advantage over her for the whole day following the night's exile. Therefore the quarrel was worth it. An advantage was, by definition, worth anything you paid for it or else it was no advantage.

He could hear her moving about in one of the other rooms and cocked an ear, satisfied. She hadn't waked him. Therefore she was about to make amends. A little itch in his spine or his brain—it was not a physical itch, so he couldn't locate it; he could only be sure that it was there—stopped troubling him momentarily; he was winning a contest. It was Glenn Tropile's nature to win contests…and his nature to create them.

Gala Tropile, young, dark, attractive, with a haunted look, came in tentatively carrying coffee from some secret hoard of hers.

Glenn Tropile affected not to notice. He stared coldly out at the cold landscape. The sea, white with thin ice, was nearly out of sight, so far had it retreated as the little sun waned.

"Glenn—"

Ah, good! *Glenn.* Where was the proper mode of first-greeting-one's-husband? Where was the prescribed throat-clearing upon entering a room?

Assiduously, he had untaught her the meticulous ritual of manners that they had all of them been brought up to know; and it was the greatest of his many victories over her that sometimes, now, *she* was the aggressor, *she* would be the first to depart from the formal behavior prescribed for Citizens.

Depravity! Perversion!

Sometimes they would touch each other at times which were not the appropriate coming-together times, Gala sitting on her husband's lap in the late evening, perhaps, or Tropile kissing her awake in the morning. Sometimes he would force her to let him watch her dress—no, not now, for the cold of the waning sun made that sort of frolic unattractive, but she had permitted it before; and such was his mastery over her that he knew she would permit it again, when the Sun was re-created....

If, a thought came to him, *if* the Sun was re-created.

* * * *

He turned away from the cold outside and looked at his wife. "Good morning, darling." She was contrite.

He demanded jarringly: "Is it?" Deliberately he stretched, deliberately he yawned, deliberately he scratched his chest. Every movement was ugly. Gala Tropile quivered, but said nothing.

Tropile flung himself on the better of the two chairs, one hairy leg protruding from under the wrapped blankets. His wife was on her best behavior—in his unique terms; she didn't avert her eyes.

"What've you got there?" he asked. "Coffee?"

"Yes, dear. I thought—"

"Where'd you get it?"

The haunted eyes looked away. Still better, thought Glenn Tropile, more satisfied even than usual; she's been ransacking an old warehouse again. It was a trick he had taught her, and like all of the illicit tricks she had learned from him, a handy weapon when he chose to use it.

It was not prescribed that a Citizen should rummage through Old Places. A Citizen did his work, whatever that work might be—banker, baker or furniture repairman. He received what rewards were his due for the work he did. A Citizen *never* took anything that was not his due—not even if it lay abandoned and rotting.

It was one of the differences between Glenn Tropile and the people he moved among.

I've got it made, he exulted; it was what I needed to clinch my victory over her.

He spoke: "I need you more than I need coffee, Gala."

She looked up, troubled.

"What would I do," he demanded, "if a beam fell on you one day while you were scrambling through the fancy groceries? How can you take such chances? Don't you *know* what you mean to me?"

She sniffed a couple of times. She said brokenly: "Darling, about last night—I'm sorry—" and miserably held out the cup. He took it and set it down. He took her hand, looked up at her, and kissed it lingeringly. He felt her tremble. Then she gave him a wild, adoring look and flung herself into his arms.

A new dominance cycle was begun at the moment he returned her frantic kisses.

Glenn knew, and Gala knew, that he had over her an edge, an advantage—the weather gauge, initiative of fire, percentage, the can't-lose lack of tension. Call it anything, but it was life itself to such as Glenn Tropile. He knew, and she knew, that having the advantage he would press it and she would yield—on and on, in a rising spiral.

He did it because it was his life, the attaining of an advantage over anyone he might encounter; because he was (unwelcomely but justly) called a Son of the Wolf.

* * * *

A world away, a Pyramid squatted sullenly on the planed-off top of the highest peak of the Himalayas.

It had not been built there. It had not been carried there by Man or Man's machines. It had—come, in its own time; for its own reasons.

Did it wake on that day, the thing atop Mount Everest, or did it ever sleep? Nobody knew. It stood, or sat, there, approximately a tetrahedron. Its appearance was known: constructed on a base line of some thirty-five yards, slaggy, midnight-blue in color. Almost nothing else about it was known—at least, to mankind.

It was the only one of its kind on Earth, though men thought (without much sure knowledge) that there were more, perhaps many thousands more, like it on the unfamiliar planet that was Earth's binary, swinging around the miniature Sun that hung at their common center of gravity like an unbalanced dumbbell. But men knew very little about that planet itself, only that it had come out of space and was now there.

Time was when men had tried to label that binary, more than two centuries before, when it had first appeared. "Runaway Planet." "The Invader." "Rejoice in Messias, the Day Is at Hand." The labels were sense-free; they were Xs in an equation, signifying only that there was *something* there which was unknown.

"The Runaway Planet" stopped running when it closed on Earth.

"The Invader" didn't invade; it merely sent down one slaggy, midnight-blue tetrahedron to Everest.

And "Rejoice in Messias" stole Earth from its sun—with Earth's old moon, which it converted into a miniature sun of its own.

That was the time when men were plentiful and strong—or thought they were—with many huge cities and countless powerful machines. It didn't matter. The new binary planet showed no interest in the cities or the machines.

There was a plague of things like Eyes—dust-devils without dust, motionless air that suddenly tensed and quivered into lenticular shapes. They came with the planet and the Pyramid, so that there probably was some connection. But there was nothing to do about the Eyes. Striking at them was like striking at air—was the same thing, in fact.

While the men and machines tried uselessly to do something about it, the new binary system—the stranger planet and Earth—began to move, accelerating very slowly.

But accelerating.

In a week, astronomers knew something was happening. In a month, the Moon sprang into flame and became a new sun—beginning to be needed, for already the parent Sol was visibly more distant, and in a few years it was only one other star among many.

* * * *

When the little sun was burned to a clinker, they—whoever "they" were, for men saw only the one Pyramid—would hang a new one in the sky. It happened every five clock-years, more or less. It was the same old moon-turned-sun, but it burned out, and the fires needed to be rekindled.

The first of these suns had looked down on an Earthly population of ten billion. As the sequence of suns waxed and waned, there were changes, climatic fluctuation, all but immeasurable differences in the quantity and kind of radiation from the new source.

The changes were such that the forty-fifth such sun looked down on a shrinking human race that could not muster up a hundred million.

A frustrated man drives inward; it is the same with a race. The hundred million that clung to existence were not the same as the bold, vital ten billion.

The thing on Everest had, in its time, received many labels, too: The Devil, The Friend, The Beast, A Pseudo-living Entity of Quite Unknown Electrochemical Properties.

All these labels were also Xs.

If it did wake that morning, it did not open its eyes, for it had no eyes—apart from the quivers of air that might or might not belong to it. Eyes might have been gouged; therefore it had none. So an illogical person might have argued—and yet it was tempting to apply the "purpose, not function" fallacy to it. Limbs could be crushed; it had no limbs. Ears could be deafened; it had none. Through a mouth, it might be poisoned; it had no mouth. Intentions and actions could be frustrated; apparently it had neither.

It was there. That was all.

It and others like it had stolen the Earth and the Earth did not know why. It was there. And the one thing on Earth you could not do was hurt it, influence it, or coerce it in any way whatever.

It was there—and it, or the masters it represented, owned the Earth by right of theft. Utterly. Beyond human hope of challenge or redress.

CHAPTER II

Citizen and Citizeness Roget Germyn walked down Pine Street in the chill and dusk of—one hoped—a Sun Re-creation Morning.

It was the convention to pretend that this was a morning like any other morning. It was not proper either to cast frequent hopeful glances at the sky, nor yet to seem disturbed or afraid because this was, after all, the forty-first such morning since those whose specialty was Sky Viewing had come to believe the Re-creation of the Sun was near.

The Citizen and his Citizeness exchanged the assurance-of-identity sign with a few old friends and stopped to converse. This also was a convention of skill divorced from purpose. The conversation was without relevance to anything that any one of the participants might know, or think, or wish to ask.

Germyn said for his friends a twenty-word poem he had made in honor of the occasion and heard their responses. They did line-capping for a while—until somebody indicated unhappiness and a wish to change by frowning the Two Grooves between his brows. The game was deftly ended with an improvised rhymed exchange.

Casually, Citizen Germyn glanced aloft. The sky-change had not begun yet; the dying old Sun hung just over the horizon, east and south, much more south than east. It was an ugly thought, but suppose, thought Germyn, just *suppose* that the Sun were not re-created today? Or tomorrow. Or—

Or ever.

The Citizen got a grip on himself and told his wife: "We shall dine at the oatmeal stall."

The Citizeness did not immediately reply. When Germyn glanced at her with well-masked surprise, he found her almost staring down the dim street at a Citizen who moved almost in a stride, almost swinging his arms. Scarcely graceful.

"That might be more Wolf than man," she said doubtfully.

Germyn knew the fellow. Tropile was his name. One of those curious few who made their homes outside of Wheeling, though they were not farmers. Germyn had had banking dealings with him—or would have had, if it had been up to Tropile.

"That is a careless man," he decided, "and an ill-bred one."

They moved toward the oatmeal stall with the gait of Citizens, arms limp, feet scarcely lifted, slumped forward a little. It was the ancient gait of fifteen hundred calories per day, not one of which could be squandered.

* * * *

There was a need for more calories. So many for walking, so many for gathering food. So many for the economical pleasures of the Citizens, so many more—oh, many more, these days!—to keep out the cold. Yet there were no more calories; the diet the whole world lived on was a bare subsistence diet.

It was impossible to farm well when half the world's land was part of the time drowned in the rising sea, part of the time smothered in falling snow.

Citizens knew this and, knowing, did not struggle—it was ungraceful to struggle, particularly when one could not win. Only—well, Wolves struggled, wasting calories, lacking grace.

Citizen Germyn turned his mind to more pleasant things.

He allowed himself his First Foretaste of the oatmeal. It would be warm in the bowl, hot in the throat, a comfort in the belly. There was a great deal of pleasure there, in weather like this, when the cold plucked through the loosened seams and the wind came up the sides of the hills. Not that there wasn't pleasure in the cold itself, for that matter. It was proper that one should be cold now, just before the re-creation of the Sun, when the old Sun was smoky-red and the new one not yet kindled.

"—still looks like Wolf to me," his wife was muttering.

"Cadence," Germyn reproved his Citizeness, but took the sting out of it with a Quirked Smile.

The man with the ugly manners was standing at the very bar of the oatmeal stall where they were heading. In the gloom of mid-morning, he was all angles and strained lines. His head was turned awkwardly on his shoulder, peering toward the back of the stall where the vendor was rhythmically measuring grain into a pot. His hands were resting helter-skelter on the counter, not hanging by his sides.

Citizen Germyn felt a faint shudder from his wife. But he did not reprove her again, for who could blame her? The exhibition was revolting.

She said faintly: "Citizen, might we dine on bread this morning?"

He hesitated and glanced again at the ugly man. He said indulgently, knowing that he was indulgent: "On Sun Re-creation Morning, the Citizeness may dine on bread." Bearing in mind the occasion, it was only a small favor and therefore a very proper one.

The bread was good, very good. They shared out the half-kilo between them and ate it in silence, as it deserved. Germyn finished his first portion and, in the prescribed pause before beginning his second, elected to refresh his eyes upward.

He nodded to his wife and stepped outside.

* * * *

Overhead, the Old Sun parceled out its last barrel-scrapings of heat. It was larger than the stars around it, but many of them were nearly as bright.

A high-pitched male voice said: "Citizen Germyn, good morning."

Germyn was caught off balance. He took his eyes off the sky, half turned, glanced at the face of the person who had spoken to him, raised his hand in the assurance-of-identity sign. It was all very quick and fluid— almost too quick, for he had had his fingers bent nearly into the sign for female friends and this was a man. Citizen Boyne. Germyn knew him well; they had shared the Ice Viewing at Niagara a year before.

Germyn recovered quickly enough, but it had been disconcerting.

He improvised swiftly: "There are stars, but are stars still there if there is no Sun?" It was a hurried effort, he grieved, but no doubt Boyne would pick it up and carry it along. Boyne had always been very good, very graceful.

Boyne did no such thing. "Good morning," he said again, faintly. He glanced at the stars overhead, as though trying to unravel what Germyn was talking about. He said accusingly, his voice cracking sharply: "There isn't any Sun, Germyn. What do you think of that?"

Germyn swallowed. "Citizen, perhaps you—"

"No Sun, you hear me!" the man sobbed. "It's cold, Germyn. The Pyramids aren't going to give us another Sun, do you know that? They're going to starve us, freeze us; they're through with us. We're done, all of us!" He was nearly screaming.

All up and down Pine Street, people were trying not to look at him and some of them were failing.

Boyne clutched at Germyn helplessly. Revolted, Germyn drew back— *bodily contact!*

It seemed to bring the man to his senses. Reason returned to his eyes. He said: "I—" He stopped, stared about him. "I think I'll have bread for breakfast," he said foolishly, and plunged into the stall.

Boyne left behind him a shaken Citizen, caught halfway into the wrist-flip of parting, staring after him with jaw slack and eyes wide, as though Germyn had no manners, either.

All this on Sun Re-creation Day!

What could it mean? Germyn wondered fretfully, worriedly.

Was Boyne on the point of—

Could Boyne be about to—

Germyn drew back from the thought. There was one thing that might explain Boyne's behavior. But it was not a proper speculation for one Citizen to make about another.

All the same—Germyn dared the thought—all the same, it *did* seem almost as though Citizen Boyne were on the point of—well, running amok.

* * * *

At the oatmeal stall, Glenn Tropile thumped on the counter. The laggard oatmeal vendor finally brought the ritual bowl of salt and the pitcher of thin milk. Tropile took his paper twist of salt from the top of the neatly arranged pile in the bowl. He glanced at the vendor. His fingers hesitated. Then, quickly, he ripped the twist of paper into his oatmeal and covered it to the permitted level with the milk.

He ate quickly and efficiently, watching the street outside.

They were wandering and mooning about, as always—maybe today more than most days, since they hoped it would be the day the Sun blossomed flame once more.

Tropile always thought of the wandering, mooning Citizens as *they*. There was a *we* somewhere for Tropile, no doubt, but Tropile had not as yet located it, not even in the bonds of the marriage contract.

He was in no hurry. At the age of fourteen, Glenn Tropile had reluctantly come to realize certain things about himself—that he disliked being bested, that he had to have a certain advantage in all his dealings, or an intolerable itch of the mind drove him to discomfort. The things added up to a terrifying fear, gradually becoming knowledge, that the only we that could properly include him was one that it was not very wise to join.

He had realized, in fact, that he was a Wolf.

For some years, Tropile had struggled against it, for Wolf was an obscene word; the children he played with were punished severely for saying it, and for almost nothing else.

It was not *proper* for one Citizen to advantage himself at the expense of another; Wolves did that.

It was *proper* for a Citizen to accept what he had, not to strive for more, to find beauty in small things, to accommodate himself, with the minimum of strain and awkwardness, to whatever his life happened to be.

Wolves were not like that. Wolves never meditated, Wolves never Appreciated, Wolves *never* were Translated—that supreme fulfillment, granted only to those who succeeded in a perfect meditation, that surrender of the world and the flesh by taking leave of both, which could never be achieved by a Wolf.

Accordingly, Glenn Tropile had tried very hard to do all the things that Wolves could not do.

He had nearly succeeded. His specialty, Water Watching, had been most rewarding. He had achieved many partly successful meditations on Connectivity.

And yet he was still a Wolf, for he still felt that burning, itching urge to triumph and to hold an advantage. For that reason, it was almost impossible for him to make friends among the Citizens; and gradually he had almost stopped trying.

Tropile had arrived in Wheeling nearly a year before, making him one of the early settlers in point of time. And yet there was not a Citizen in the street who was prepared to exchange recognition gestures with him.

He knew *them*, nearly every one. He knew their names and their wives' names. He knew what northern states they had moved down from with the spreading of the ice, as the sun grew dim. He knew very nearly to the quarter of a gram what stores of sugar and salt and coffee each one of them had put away—for their guests, of course, not for themselves; the well-bred Citizen hoarded only for the entertainment of others.

Tropile knew these things because there was an advantage in knowing them. But there was no advantage in having anyone know him.

A few did—that banker, Germyn; Tropile had approached him only a few months before about a prospective loan. But it had been a chancy, nervous encounter. The idea was so luminously simple to Tropile—organize an expedition to the coal mines that once had flourished nearby, find the coal, bring it to Wheeling, heat the houses. And yet it had seemed blasphemous to Germyn. Tropile had counted himself lucky merely to have been refused the loan, instead of being cried out upon as Wolf.

* * * *

The oatmeal vendor was fussing worriedly around his neat stack of paper twists in the salt bowl.

Tropile avoided the man's eyes. Tropile was not interested in the little wry smile of self-deprecation which the vendor would make to him, given half a chance. Tropile knew well enough what was disturbing the vendor. Let it disturb him. It was Tropile's custom to take extra twists of salt. They were in his pockets now; they would stay there. Let the vendor wonder why he was short.

Tropile licked the bowl of his spoon and stepped into the street. He was comfortably aware under a double-thick parka that the wind was blowing very cold.

A Citizen passed him, walking alone: odd, thought Tropile. He was walking rapidly and there was a look of taut despair on his face. Still more odd. Odd enough to be worth another look, because that sort of haste, that sort of abstraction, suggested something to Tropile. They were in no way normal to the gentle sheep of the class *They*, except in one particular circumstance.

Glenn Tropile crossed the street to follow the abstracted Citizen, whose name, he knew, was Boyne. The man blundered into Citizen Germyn outside the baker's stall, and Tropile stood back out of easy sight, watching and listening.

Boyne was on the ragged edge of breakdown. What Tropile heard and saw confirmed his diagnosis. The one particular circumstance was close to happening—Citizen Boyne was on the verge of running amok.

Tropile looked at the man with amusement and contempt. Amok! The gentle sheep *could* be pushed too far. He had seen Citizens run amok, the signs were obvious.

There was pretty sure to be an advantage in it for Glenn Tropile. There was an advantage in almost anything, if you looked for it.

He watched and waited. He picked his spot with care, so that he could see Citizen Boyne inside the baker's stall, making a dismal botch of slashing his quarter-kilo of bread from the Morning Loaf.

He waited for Boyne to come racing out....

Boyne did.

A yell—loud, piercing. It was Citizen Germyn, shrilling: "Amok, amok!" A scream. An enraged wordless cry from Boyne, and the baker's knife glinting in the faint light as Boyne swung it. And then Citizens were scattering in every direction—all of the Citizens but one.

One Citizen was under the knife—his own knife, as it happened; it was the baker himself. Boyne chopped and chopped again. And then Boyne came out, roaring, the broad knife whistling about his head. The gentle Citizens fled panicked before him. He struck at their retreating forms and screamed and struck again. Amok.

It was the one particular circumstance when they forgot to be gracious—one of the two, Tropile corrected himself as he strolled across to the baker's stall. His brow furrowed, because there was another circumstance when they lacked grace, and one which affected him nearly.

* * * *

He watched the maddened creature, Boyne, already far down the road, chasing a knot of Citizens around a corner. Tropile sighed and stepped into the baker's stall to see what he might gain from this.

Boyne would wear himself out—the surging rage would leave him as quickly as it came; he would be a sheep again and the other sheep would close in and capture him. That was what happened when a Citizen ran amok. It was a measure of what pressures were on the Citizens that, at any moment, there might be one gram of pressure too much and one of them would crack. It had happened here in Wheeling twice within the past two months. Glenn Tropile had seen it happen in Pittsburgh, Altoona and Bronxville.

There is a limit to the pressure that can be endured.

Tropile walked into the baker's stall and looked down without emotion at the slaughtered baker. The corpse was a gory mess, but Tropile had seen corpses before.

He looked around the stall, calculating. As a starter, he bent to pick up the quarter-kilo of bread Boyne had dropped, dusted it off and slipped it into his pocket. Food was always useful. Given enough food, perhaps Boyne would not have run amok.

Was it simple hunger they cracked under? Or the knowledge of the thing on Mount Everest, or the hovering Eyes, or the sought-after-dreaded prospect of Translation, or merely the strain of keeping up their laboriously figured lives?

Did it matter? *They* cracked and ran amok, and Tropile never would, and that was what mattered.

He leaned across the counter, reaching for what was left of the Morning Loaf—

And found himself staring into the terrified large eyes of Citizeness Germyn.

She screamed: "Wolf! Citizens, help me! Wolf!"

Tropile faltered. He hadn't even *seen* the damned woman, but there she was, rising up from behind the counter, screaming her head off: "Wolf! Wolf!"

He said sharply: "Citizeness, I beg you—" But that was no good. The evidence was on him and her screams would fetch others.

Tropile panicked. He started toward her to silence her, but that was no good, either. He whirled. She was screaming, screaming, and there were people to hear. Tropile darted into the street, but they were popping out of every doorway now, appearing from each rat's hole in which they had hid to escape Boyne.

"Please!" he cried, sobbing. "Wait a minute!"

But they weren't waiting. They had heard the woman and maybe some of them had seen him with the bread. They were all around him—no, they were all over him; they were clutching at him, tearing at his soft, warm furs.

They pulled at his pockets and the stolen twists of salt spilled accusingly out. They yanked at his sleeves and even the stout, unweakened seams ripped open. He was fairly captured.

"Wolf!" they were shouting. "Wolf!" It drowned out the distant noise from where Boyne had finally been run to earth, a block and more away. It drowned out everything.

It was the other circumstance when *they* forgot to be gracious: when they had trapped a Son of the Wolf.

CHAPTER III

Engineering had long ago come to an end.

Engineering is possible under one condition of the equation: Total available Calories divided by Population equals Artistic-Technological Style. When the ratio Calories-to-Population is large—say, five thousand or more, five thousand daily calories for every living person—then the Artistic-Technological Style is *big*. People carve Mount Rushmore; they build great foundries; they manufacture enormous automobiles to carry one housewife half a mile for the purchase of one lipstick.

Life is coarse and rich where C:P is large. At the other extreme, where C:P is too small, life does not exist at all. It has starved out.

Experimentally, add little increments to C:P and it will be some time before the right-hand side of the equation becomes significant. But at last, in the 1,000 to 1,500 calorie range, Artistic-Technological Style firmly appears in self-perpetuating form. C:P in that range produces the small arts, the appreciations, the peaceful arrangements of necessities into subtle relationships of traditionally agreed-upon virtue.

Think of Japan, locked into its Shogunate prison, with a hungry population scrabbling food out of mountainsides and beauty out of arrangements of lichens. The small, inexpensive sub-sub-arts are characteristic of the 1,000 to 1,500 calorie range.

And this was the range of Earth, the world of ten billion men, when the planet was stolen by its new binary.

Some few persons inexpensively studied the study of science with pencil and renewable paper, but the last research accelerator had long since been shut down. The juice from its hydro-power dam was needed to supply meager light to a million homes and to cook the pablum for two million brand-new babies.

In those days, one dedicated Byzantine wrote the definitive encyclopedia of engineering (though he was no engineer). Its four hundred and twenty tiny volumes examined exhaustively the engineering feats of ancient Greece and Egypt, the Wall of Shih-Hwang Ti, the Gothic builders, Brunel who changed the face of England, the Roeblings of Brooklyn, Groves of the Pentagon, Duggan of the Shelter System (before C:P dropped to the point where war became vanishingly implausible), Levern of Operation Up. But the encyclopedist could not use a slide rule without thinking, faltering, jotting down his decimals.

And then…the magnitudes grew less.

Under the tectonic and climatic battering of the great abduction of Earth from its primary, under the sine-wave advances to and retreats from the equator of the ice sheath, as the small successor Suns waxed, waned, died and were replaced, the ratio C:P remained stable. C had diminished enormously; so had P. As the calories to support life grew scarce, so the consuming mouths of mankind grew less in number.

* * * *

The forty-fifth small Sun shone on no engineers.

Not even on the binary, perhaps. The Pyramids, the things on the binary, the thing on Mount Everest—they were not engineers. They employed a crude metaphysic based on dissection and shoving.

They had no elegant field theories. All they knew was that everything came apart, and that if you pushed a thing, it would move.

If your biggest push would not move a thing, you took it apart and pushed the parts, and then it would move. Sometimes, for nuclear effects, they had to take things apart into 3×10^9 pieces and shove each piece very carefully.

By taking apart and shoving, then, they landed their one spaceship on the burned-out sunlet. Four human beings were on that ship. They meditated briefly on Connectivity and died screaming.

A point of new flame appeared on the sunlet's surface and the spaceship scrambled for the binary. The point of flame went from cherry through orange into the blue-white and began to spread.

* * * *

At the moment of the Re-creation of the Sun, there was rejoicing on the Earth.

Not quite everywhere, though. In Wheeling's House of the Five Regulations, Glenn Tropile waited unquietly for death. Citizen Boyne, who had run amok and slaughtered the baker, shared Tropile's room and his doom, but not his rage. Boyne, with demure pleasure, was composing his death poem.

"Talk to me!" snapped Tropile. "Why are we here? What did you do and why did you do it? What have I done? Why don't I pick up a bench and kill you with it? You would've killed me two hours ago if I'd caught your eye!"

There was no satisfaction in Citizen Boyne; the passions were burned out of him. He politely tendered Tropile a famous aphorism: "Citizen, the art of living is the substitution of unimportant, answerable questions for important, unanswerable ones. Come, let us appreciate the new-born Sun."

He turned to the window, where the spark of blue-white flame in what had once been the crater of Tycho was beginning to spread across the charred moon.

Tropile was child enough of his culture to turn with him, almost involuntarily. He was silent. That blue-white infinitesimal up there growing slowly—the oneness, the calm rapture of Being in a universe that you shaded into without harsh discontinua, the being one with the great blue-white gem-flower blossoming now in the heavens that were no different stuff than you yourself—

He closed his eyes, calm, and meditated on Connectivity.

He was being Good.

By the time the fusion reaction had covered the whole small disk of the sunlet, a quarter-hour at the most, his meditation began to wear off.

Tropile shrugged out of his torn parka, not bothering to rip it further. It was already growing warm in the room. Citizen Boyne, of course, was carefully opening every seam with graceful rending motions, miming great and smooth effort of the biceps and trapezius.

But the meditation was over, and as Tropile watched his cellmate, he screamed a silent *Why?* Since his adolescence, that wailing syllable had seldom been far from his mind. It could be silenced by appreciation and meditation.

Tropile's specialty was Water Watching and he was so good at it that several beginners had asked him for instruction in the subtle art, in spite of his notorious oddities of life and manner. He *enjoyed* Water Watching. He almost pitied anybody so single-mindedly devoted to, say, Clouds and Odors—great game though it was—that he had never even tried Water Watching. And after a session of Watching, when one was lucky enough to observe the Nine Boiling Stages in classic perfection, one might slip into meditation and be harmonious, feel Good.

But what did one do when the meditations failed, as they had failed him? What did one do when they came farther and farther apart, became less and less intense, could be inspired, finally, only by a huge event like the renewal of the Sun?

One went amok, he had always thought.

But he had not. Boyne had. He had been declared a Son of the Wolf, on no evidence that he could understand. Yet he had not run amok.

Still, the penalties were the same, he thought, uncomfortably aware of an unfamiliar itch—not the inward intolerable itch of needing the advantage, but a localized sensation at the base of his spine. The penalties for all gross crimes—Wolfhood or running amok—were the same, and simply this:

They would perform the Lumbar Puncture. He would make the Donation of Spinal Fluid.

He would be dead.

* * * *

The Keeper of the House of Five Regulations, an old man, Citizen Harmane, looked in on his charges—approvingly at Boyne, with a beclouded expression at Glenn Tropile.

It was thought that even Wolves were entitled to the common human decencies in the brief interval between exposure and the Donation of Fluid. The Keeper would not have dreamed of scowling at the detected Wolf or of interfering with whatever wretched imitation of meditation-before-dying the creature might practice. But he could not, all the same, bring himself to offer even an assurance-of-identity gesture.

Tropile had no such qualms.

He scowled at Keeper Harmane with such ferocity that the old man almost hurried away. He turned an almost equally ugly scowl upon Citizen Boyne. How dared that knife-murderer be so calm, so relaxed!

Tropile said brutally: "They'll kill us! You know that? They'll stick a needle in our spines and drain us dry. It *hurts*. Do you understand me? They're going to drain us, and then they're going to drink our spinal fluid, and it's going to *hurt*."

He was gently corrected. "We shall make the Donation," Citizen Boyne said calmly. "Is not the difference intelligible to a Son of the Wolf?"

True culture demanded that that remark be accepted as a friendly joke, probably based on a truth—how else could an unpalatable truth be put in words? Otherwise the unthinkable might happen. They might quarrel. They might even come to blows!

The appropriate mild smile formed on Tropile's lips, but harshly he wiped it off. They were going to *kill* him. He would *not* smile for them! And the effort was enormous.

"I'm *not* a Son of the Wolf!" he howled, desperate, knowing he was protesting to the man of all men in Wheeling who didn't care, and who could do least about it if he did. "What's this crazy talk about Wolves? I don't know what a Son of the Wolf is and I don't think you or anybody does. All I know is that I was acting *sensibly*. And everybody began howling! You're supposed to know a Son of the Wolf by his unculture, his ignorance, his violence. But you chopped down three people and I only picked up a piece of bread! And *I'm* supposed to be the dangerous one!"

"Wolves never know they're Wolves," sighed Citizen Boyne. "Fish probably think they're birds and you evidently think you're a Citizen. Would a Citizen speak as you are speaking?"

"But they're going to kill us!"

"Then why aren't you composing your death poem?"

* * * *

Glenn Tropile took a deep breath. Something was biting him. It was bad enough that he was about to die, bad enough that he had done nothing worth dying for. But what was gnawing at him now had nothing to do with dying.

The percentages were going the wrong way. This pale Citizen was getting an edge on him.

An engorged gland in Tropile's adrenals—it was only a pinhead in Citizen Boyne's—gushed raw hormones into his bloodstream. He could die, yes—that was a skill everyone had to acquire, sooner or later. But while he was alive, he could not stand to be bested in an encounter, an argument, a relationship—not and stay alive. Wolf? Call him Wolf. Call him Operator, or Percentage Player; call him Sharp Article; call him Gamesman.

If there was an advantage to be derived, he would derive it. It was the way he was put together.

He said, for time: "You're right. Stupid of me. I must have lost my head!"

He thought. Some men think by poking problems apart; some think by laying facts side by side to compare. Tropile's thinking was neither of these, but a species of judo. He conceded to his opponent such things as Strength, Armor, Resource. He didn't need these things for himself; to every contest, the opponent brought enough of them to supply two. It was Tropile's habit (and Wolfish, he had to admit) to use the opponent's strength against him, to break the opponent against his own steel walls.

He thought.

The first thing was to make up his mind: He was Wolf. Then let him *be* Wolf. He wouldn't stay around for the spinal tap; he would go from there. But how?

The second thing was to plan. There were obstacles. Citizen Boyne was one. The Keeper of the House of the Five Regulations was another.

Where was the pole which would permit him to vault over these hurdles? There was always his wife, Gala. He owned her; she would do what he wished—provided he made her *want* to do it.

Yes, Gala. He walked to the door and shouted to Citizen Harmane: "Keeper! I must see my wife! Have her brought to me!"

It was impossible for the Keeper to refuse. He called gently, "I will invite the Citizeness," and toddled away.

The third thing was time.

Tropile turned to Citizen Boyne. "Citizen," he said persuasively, "since your death poem is ready and mine is not, will you be gracious enough to go first when they—when they come?"

Citizen Boyne looked temperately at his cellmate and made the Quirked Smile.

"You see?" he said. "Wolf."

And that was true. But what was also true was that Boyne couldn't and didn't refuse.

CHAPTER IV

Half a world away, the midnight-blue Pyramid sat on its planed-off peak as it had sat since the days when Earth had a real sun of its own.

It was of no importance to the Pyramid that Glenn Tropile was about to receive a slim catheter into his spine, to drain his saps and his life. It didn't matter to the Pyramid that the pretext for the execution was an act which human history had long stopped considering a capital crime. Ritual sacrifice in any guise made no difference to the Pyramid.

The Pyramid saw them come and the Pyramid saw them go—if the Pyramid could be said to "see." One human being more or less, what matter? Who bothers to take a census of the cells in a hangnail?

And yet the Pyramid did have a kind of interest in Glenn Tropile. Or, at least, in the human race of which he was a part.

Nobody knew much about the Pyramids, but everybody knew *that* much. They wanted something—else why would they have bothered to steal the Earth?

The date of the theft was 2027. A great year—the year of the first landings on the Runaway Planet that had come blundering into the Solar System. Maybe those landings were a mistake—although they were a very great triumph, too; but maybe if it hadn't been for the landings, the Runaway Planet might have run right through the ecliptic and away.

However, the triumphal mistake was made and that was the first time a human eye saw a Pyramid.

Shortly after—though not before a radio message was sent—that human eye winked out forever; but by then the damage was done. What passed in a Pyramid for "attention" had been attracted. The next thing that happened set the wireless channels between Palomar and Pernambuco, between Greenwich and the Cape of Good Hope, buzzing and worrying, as astronomers all over the Earth reported and confirmed and reconfirmed the astonishing fact that our planet was on the move. Rejoice in Messias had come to take us away.

A world of ten billion people, some of them brilliant, many of them brave, built and flung the giant rockets of Operation Up at the invader: Nothing.

The first, and only, Interplanetary Expeditionary Force was boosted up to no-gravity and dropped onto the new planet to strike back: Nothing.

Earth moved spirally outward.

If a battle could not be won, then perhaps a migration. New ships were built in haste. But they lay there rusting as the sun grew small and the ice grew thick, because where was there to go? Not Mars. Not the Moon, which was trailing alone. Not choking Venus or crushing Jupiter.

The migration was defeated as surely as the war, there being no place to migrate to.

One Pyramid came to Earth, only one. It shaved the crest off the highest mountain there was and squatted on it. An observer? A warden? Whatever it was, it stayed.

The sun grew too distant to be of use, and out of the old Moon, the Pyramid aliens built a new small sun in the sky—a five-year sun that burned out and was replaced, again and again and endlessly again.

It had been a fierce struggle against unbeatable odds on the part of the ten billion; and when the uselessness of struggle was demonstrated at last, many of the ten billion froze to death, and many of them starved, and nearly all of the rest had something frozen or starved out of them; and what was left, two centuries and more later, was more or less like Citizen Boyne, except for a few—a very few—like Glenn Tropile.

* * * *

Gala Tropile stared miserably at her husband. "I want to get out of here," he was saying urgently. "They mean to kill me. Gala, you know you can't make yourself suffer by letting them kill me!"

She wailed: "I *can't!*"

Tropile looked over his shoulder. Citizen Boyne was fingering the textured contrasts of a golden watch-case which had been his father's—and soon would be his son's. Boyne's eyes were closed and he wasn't listening.

Tropile leaned forward and deliberately put his hand on his wife's arm. She started and flushed, of course.

"You *can*," he said, "and what's more, you will. You can help me get out of here. I insist on it, Gala, because I must save you that pain."

He took his hand off her arm, content.

He said harshly: "Darling, don't you think I know how much we've always meant to each other?"

She looked at him wretchedly. Fretfully she tore at the billowing filmy sleeve of her summer blouse. The seams hadn't been loosened; there had not been time. She had just been getting into the appropriate Sun Re-creation Day costume, to be worn under the parka, when the messenger had come with the news about her husband.

She avoided his eyes. "If you're really Wolf...."

Tropile's sub-adrenals pulsed and filled him with confident strength. "*You* know what I am—you better than anyone else." It was a sly reminder of their curious furtive behavior together; like the hand on her arm, it had its effect. "After all, why do we quarrel the way we did last night?"

He hurried on; the job of the rowel was to spur her to action, not to inflame a wound. "Because we're *important* to each other. I know that you would count on me to help if you were in trouble. And I know that you'd be hurt—*deeply*, Gala!—if I didn't count on you."

She sniffled and scuffed the bright strap over her open-toed sandal.

Then she met his eyes.

It was the after-effect of the argument, of course. Glenn Tropile knew just how heavily he could rely on the after-spiral of a quarrel. She was submitting.

She glanced furtively at Citizen Boyne and lowered her voice.

"What do I have to do?" she whispered.

* * * *

In five minutes, she was gone, but that was more than enough time. Tropile had at least thirty minutes left. They would take Boyne first; he had seen to that. And once Boyne was gone—

Tropile wrenched a leg off his three-legged stool and sat precariously balanced on the other two. He tossed the loose leg clattering into a corner.

The Keeper of the House of Five Regulations ambled slack-bodied by and glanced into the room. "Wolf, what happened to your stool?"

Tropile made a left-handed sign of no-importance. "It doesn't matter. Except it *is* hard to meditate, sitting on this thing, with every muscle tensing and fighting against every other to keep my balance...."

The Keeper made an overruling sign of please-let-me-help. "It's your last half-hour, Wolf," he reminded Tropile. "I'll fix the stool for you."

He entered and slammed and banged it together, and left with an expression of mild concern. Even a Son of the Wolf was entitled to the fullest appreciation of that unique opportunity for meditation, the last half-hour before a Donation.

In five minutes, the Keeper was back, looking solemn and yet glad, like a bearer of serious but welcome tidings.

"It is the time for the first Donation," he announced. "Which of you—"

"Him," said Tropile quickly, pointing.

Boyne opened his eyes calmly and nodded. He got to his feet, made a formal leavetaking bow to Tropile, and followed the Keeper toward his Donation and his death. As they were going out, Tropile coughed a would-you-please-grant-me-a-favor cough.

The Keeper paused. "What is it, Wolf?"

Tropile showed him the empty water pitcher—empty, all right; he had emptied it out the window.

"My apologies," the Keeper said, flustered, and hurried Boyne along. He came back almost at once to fill the pitcher, even though he should be there to watch Boyne's ceremonial Donation.

Tropile stood looking at the Keeper, his sub-adrenals beginning to pound like the rolling boil of Well-aged Water. The Keeper was at a disadvantage. He had been neglectful of his charge—a broken stool, no water in the pitcher. And a Citizen, brought up in a Citizen's maze of consideration and tact, could not help but be humiliated, seeking to make amends.

Tropile pressed his advantage home. "Wait," he said to the Keeper. "I'd like to talk to you."

The Keeper hesitated, torn. "The Donation—"

"Damn the Donation," Tropile said calmly. "After all, what is it but sticking a pipe into a man's backbone and sucking out the juice that keeps him alive? It's killing, that's all."

The Keeper turned literally white. Tropile was speaking blasphemy and he wasn't stopping.

"I want to tell you about my wife," Tropile went on, assuming a confidential air. "Now there's a real *woman*. Not one of these frozen-up Citizenesses, you know? Why, she and I used to—" He hesitated. "You're a man of the world, aren't you?" he demanded. "I mean you've seen life."

"I—suppose so," the Keeper said faintly.

"Then you won't be shocked," Tropile lied. "Well, let me tell you, there's a lot to women that these stuffed-shirt Citizens don't know about. Boy! Ever see a woman's knee?" He sniggered. "Ever kiss a woman with—" he winked—"with the *light on*? Ever sit in a big armchair, say, with a woman in your *lap*—all soft and heavy, and kind of warm, and slumped up against your chest, you know, and—"

He stopped and swallowed. He was almost making himself retch, it was so hard to say these things. But he forced himself to go on: "Well, that's what she and I used to do. Plenty. All the time. That's what I call a real *woman*."

He stopped, warned by the Keeper's sudden change of expression, glazed eyes, strangling breath. He had gone too far. He had only wanted to paralyze the man, revolt him, put him out of commission, but he was overdoing it. He jumped forward and caught the Keeper as he fell, fainting.

* * * *

Tropile callously emptied the water pitcher over the man. The Keeper sneezed and sat up groggily. He focused his eyes on Tropile and agonizedly blushed.

Tropile said harshly: "I wish to see the new sun from the street."

The request was incredible. Even after the unbelievable obscenities he had heard, the Keeper was not prepared for this; he was staggered. Tropile was in detention regarding the Fifth Regulation. That was all there was to it. Such persons were not to be released from their quarters. The Keeper knew it, the world knew it, Tropile knew it.

It was an obscenity even greater than the lurid tales of perverted lust, for Tropile had asked something which was impossible! No one *ever* asked anything that was impossible to grant, for no one could ever refuse anything. That was utterly graceless, unthinkable.

One could only attempt to compromise. The Keeper stammeringly said: "May I—may I let you see the new sun from the corridor?" And even that was wretchedly wrong, but he had to offer something. One always offered something. The Keeper had never since babyhood given a flat no to anybody about anything. No Citizen had. A flat no led to anger, strong words—perhaps even hurt feelings. The only flat no conceivable was the enormous terminal no of an amok. Short of that—

One offered. One split the difference. One was invariably filled with tepid pleasure when, invariably, the offer was accepted, the difference was split, both parties were satisfied.

"That will do for a start," Tropile snarled. "Open, man, open! Don't make me wait."

The Keeper reeled and unlatched the door to the corridor.

"Now the street!"

"I can't!" burst in an anguished cry from the Keeper. He buried his face in his hands and began to sob, hopelessly incapacitated.

"The street!" Tropile said remorselessly. He himself felt wrenchingly ill; he was going against custom that had ruled his own life as surely as the Keeper's.

But he was Wolf. "I *will* be Wolf," he growled, and advanced upon the Keeper. "My wife," he said, "I didn't finish telling you. Sometimes she used to put her arm around me and just snuggle up and—I remember one time she kissed my ear. Broad daylight. It felt funny and warm—I can't describe it."

Whimpering, the Keeper flung the keys at Tropile and tottered brokenly away.

He was out of the action. Tropile himself was nearly as badly off; the difference was that he continued to function. The words coming from him had seared like acid in his throat.

"They call me Wolf," he said aloud, reeling against the wall. "I will be one."

He unlocked the outer door and his wife was waiting, holding in her arms the things he had asked her to bring.

Tropile said strangely to her: "I am steel and fire. I am Wolf, full of the old moxie."

She wailed: "Glenn, are you sure I'm doing the right thing?"

He laughed unsteadily and led her by the arm through the deserted streets.

CHAPTER V

Citizen Germyn, as was his right by position and status as a connoisseur, helped prepare Citizen Boyne for his Donation. There was nothing much to it—which made it an elaborate and lengthy task, according to the ethic of the Citizens; it had to be protracted, each step being surrounded by fullest dress of ritual.

It was done in the broad daylight of the new Sun, and as many of the three hundred citizens of Wheeling as could manage it were in the courtyard of the old Federal Building to watch.

The nature of the ceremony was this: A man who revealed himself Wolf, or who finally crumbled under the demands of life and ran amok, could not be allowed to live. He was hauled before an audience of his equals and permitted—with the help of regretful force, if that should be necessary, but preferably not—to make the Donation of Spinal Fluid.

Execution was murder and murder was not permitted under the gentle code of Citizens; this was not execution. The draining of a man's spinal fluid did not kill him. It only insured that, after a time and with much suffering, his internal chemistry would so arrange itself that it would continue to function, only not in a way that would sustain life.

Once the Donation was made, the problem was completely altered, of course. Suffering was bad in itself. To save the Donor from the suffering that lay ahead, it was the custom to have the oldest and gentlest Citizen on hand stand by with a sharp-edged knife. When the Donation was complete, the Donor's head was removed—purely to avert suffering. That was not execution, either, but only the hastening of an inevitable end.

The dozen or so Citizens whose rank permitted them to assist then dissolved the spinal fluids in water and ceremoniously sipped them, at which time it was proper to offer a small poem in commentary. All in all, it was a perfectly splendid opportunity for the purest form of meditation for everyone concerned.

Citizen Germyn, whose role was Catheter Bearer, took his place behind the Introducer Bearer, the Annunciators and the Questioner of Purpose. As he passed Citizen Boyne, Germyn assisted him to assume the proper crouched-over position. Boyne looked up gratefully and Germyn found the occasion correct for a commendatory half-smile.

The Questioner of Purpose said solemnly to Boyne: "It is your privilege to make a Donation here today. Do you wish to do so?"

"I do," said Boyne raptly. The anxiety had passed; clearly he was confident of making a good Donation. Germyn approved with all his heart.

The Annunciators, in alternate stanzas, announced the right pause for meditation to the meager crowd, and all fell silent. Citizen Germyn began the process of blanking out his mind, to ready himself for the great opportunity to Appreciate that lay ahead. A sound distracted him; he glanced up irritably. It seemed to come from the House of the Five Regulations, a man's voice, carrying. But no one else appeared to notice it. All of the watchers, all of those on the stone steps, were in somber meditation.

Germyn tried to return his thoughts to where they belonged.

But something was troubling him. He had caught a glimpse of the Donor and there had been something—something—

He angrily permitted himself to look up once more to see just what it had been about Citizen Boyne that had attracted his attention.

Yes, there *was* something. Over the form of Citizen Boyne, silent, barely visible, a flicker of life and motion. Nothing tangible. It was as if the air itself were in motion.

It was, Germyn thought with a bursting heart—it was an Eye!

The veritable miracle of Translation and it was about to take place here and now, upon the person of Citizen Boyne! And no one knew it but Germyn himself!

* * * *

In this last surmise, Citizen Germyn was wrong. Or was he? True, no other human eyes saw the flawed-glass thing that twisted the air over Boyne's prostrate body, but there was, in a sense, another witness…some thousands of miles away.

The Pyramid on Mount Everest "stirred."

It did not move, but something about it moved, or changed, or radiated. The Pyramid surveyed its—cabbage patch? Wristwatch mine? As much sense, it may be, to say wristwatch patch or cabbage mine. At any rate, it surveyed what to it was a place where intricate mechanisms grew, ripened and were dug up at the moment of usefulness, whereupon they were quick-frozen and wired into circuits.

Through signals perceptible to it, the Pyramids had become "aware" that one of its mechanisms was now ready to be plucked—harvested.

The Pyramid's blood was dielectric fluid. Its limbs were electrostatic charges. Its philosophy was: Unscrew It and Push. Its motive was survival.

Survival today was not what survival once had been, for a Pyramid.

Once survival had merely been gliding along on a cushion of repellent charges, streaming electrons behind for the push, sending h-f pulses out often enough to get a picture of their bounced return to integrate deep inside.

If the picture showed something metabolizable, one metabolized it. One broke it down into molecules by lashing it with the surplus protons left over from the dispersed electrons; one adsorbed the molecules. Sometimes the metabolizable object was an Immobile and sometimes a Mobile—a vague, theoretical, frivolous classification to a philosophy whose basis was that *everything* unscrewed. If it was a Mobile, one sometimes had to move after it.

That was the difference.

The essential was survival, not making idle distinctions. And one small part of survival today was the Everest Pyramid's job.

It sat and waited. It sent out its h-f pulses bouncing and scattering, and it bounced and scattered them additionally on their return. Deep inside, the more-than-anamorphically distorted picture was reintegrated. Deeper inside, it was interpreted and evaluated for its part in survival.

* * * *

There was a need for certain mechanisms which grew on this planet. At irregular times, the Pyramid evaluated the picture to the effect that a mechanism—a wristwatch, so to speak—was ripe for plucking; and by electrostatic charges, it did so. The electrostatic charges, in forming, produced what humans called an Eye. But the Pyramid had no use for names.

It merely plucked, when a mechanism was ripe. It had found that a mechanism was ripe now.

A world away, before the steps of Wheeling's Federal Building, electrostatic charges gathered above a component whose name was Citizen Boyne. There was a small sound like the clapping of two hands which made the three hundred citizens of Wheeling jerk upright out of their meditations.

The sound was air filling the gap that had once been occupied by Citizen Boyne, who had instantly vanished—who had, in a word, been ripe and therefore been plucked.

CHAPTER VI

Glenn Tropile and his sobbing wife passed the night in the stubble of a cornfield. Neither of them slept much.

Tropile, numbed by contact with the iron chill of the field—it would be months before the new Sun warmed the Earth enough for it to begin radiating in turn—tossed restlessly, dreaming. He was Wolf. Let it be so, he told himself again and again. I *will* be Wolf. I will strike back at the Citizens. I will—

Always the thought trailed off. He would exactly *What*? What could he do?

Migration was an answer—go to another city. With Gala, he guessed. Start a new life, where he was not known as Wolf.

And then what? Try to live a sheep's life, as he had tried all his years? And there was the question of whether, in fact, he could manage to find a city where he was not known. The human race was migratory, in these years of subjection to the never quite understood rule of the Pyramids.

It was a matter of insulation. When the new Sun was young, it was hot, and there was plenty of warmth; it was possible to spread north and south, away from final line of permafrost which, in North America, came just above the old Mason-Dixon line. When the Sun was dying, the cold spread down. The race followed the seasons. Soon all of Wheeling would be spreading north again, and how was he to be sure that none of Wheeling's Citizens might not turn up wherever he might go?

He could be sure—that was the answer to that.

All right, scratch migration. What remained? He could—with Gala, he guessed—live a solitary life on the fringes of cultivated land. They both had some skill at rummaging the old storehouses of the ancients, and there was still food and other commodities to be found.

But even a Wolf is gregarious by nature and there were bleak hours in that night when Tropile found himself close to sobbing with his wife.

At the first break of dawn, he was up. Gala had fallen into a light and restless sleep; he called her awake.

"We have to move," he said harshly. "Maybe they'll get up enough guts to follow us. I don't want them to find us."

Silently she got up. They rolled and tied the blankets she had bought; they ate quickly from the food she had brought; they made packs and put them on their shoulders and started to walk. One thing in their favor: they were moving fast, faster than any Citizen was likely to follow. All the same, Tropile kept looking nervously behind him.

They hurried north and east, and that was a mistake, because by noon they found themselves blocked by water. Once it had been a river; the melting of the polar ice caps that had submerged the coasts of the old continents had drowned it out and now it was salt water. But whatever it was, it was impassable. They would have to skirt it westward until they found a bridge or a boat.

"We can stop and eat," Tropile said grudgingly, trying not to despair.

They slumped to the ground. It was warmer now. Tropile found himself getting drowsier, drowsier—

He jerked erect and stared around belligerently. Beside him, his wife was lying motionless, though her eyes were open, gazing at the sky. Tropile sighed and stretched out. A moment's rest, he promised himself, and then a quick bite to eat, and then onward....

He was sound asleep when they spotted him.

* * * *

There was a flutter of iron bird's wings from overhead. Tropile jumped up out of his sleep, awakening to panic. It was outside the possibility of belief, but there it was:

In the sky over him, etched black against a cloud, a helicopter. And men staring out of it, staring down at him.

A helicopter!

But there were no helicopters, or none that flew—if there had been fuel to fly them with—if any man had had the skill to make them fly. It was impossible! And yet there it was, and the men were looking at him, and the impossible great whirling thing was coming down, nearer.

He began to run in the downward wash of air from the vanes. But it was no use. There were three men and they were fresh and he wasn't. He stopped, dropping into the fighter's crouch that is pre-set into the human body, ready to do battle.

The men didn't want to fight. They laughed and one of them said amiably: "*Long* past your bedtime, boy. Get in. We'll take you home."

Tropile stood poised, hands half-clenched. "Take—"

"Take you home. Yeah. Where you belong, Tropile. Not back to Wheeling, if that's what is worrying you."

"Where I—"

"Where you belong."

Then Tropile understood.

He got into the helicopter wonderingly. Home. So there *was* a home for such as he. He wasn't alone. He needn't keep his solitary self apart. He could be with his own kind.

He remembered Gala Tropile and paused. One of the men said with quick understanding: "Your wife? I think we saw her about half a mile from here. Heading back to Wheeling as fast as she could go."

Tropile nodded. That was better, after all. Gala was no Wolf, though he had tried his best to make her one.

One of the men closed the door; another did something with levers and wheels; the vanes whooshed around overhead; the helicopter bounced on its stiff-sprung landing legs and then rocked up and away.

For the first time in his life, Glenn Tropile looked *down* on the land.

They didn't fly high—but Glenn Tropile had never flown at all, and the two or three hundred feet of air beneath made him faint and queasy. They danced through the passes in the West Virginia hills, crossed icy streams and rivers, swung past old empty towns which no longer even had names of their own. They saw no one.

It was something over four hundred miles to where they were going, one of the men told him. They made it easily before dark.

* * * *

As Tropile walked through the town in the evening light, electricity flared white and violet in the buildings around him. Imagine! Electricity was calories, and calories were to be hoarded.

There were other walkers in the street. Their gait was not the economical shuffle with pendant arms. They burned energy visibly. They swung. They *strode*. It had been chiseled on his brain in earliest childhood that such walking was wrong, reprehensible, debilitating. It wasted calories. These people did not look debilitated and they didn't seem to mind wasting calories.

It was an ordinary sort of town, apparently named Princeton. It did not have the transient look to it of, say, Wheeling, or Altoona, or Gary, in Tropile's experience. It looked like—well, it looked permanent.

Tropile had heard of a town called Princeton, but it happened that he had never passed through it southwarding or northbound. There was no reason why he or anybody should or should not have. Still, there was a possibility, once he thought of it, that things were somehow so arranged that they should not; maybe it was all on purpose. Like every town, it was underpopulated, but not so much so as most. Perhaps one living space in five was used. A high ratio.

The man beside him was named Haendl, one of the men from the helicopter. They hadn't talked much on the flight and they didn't talk much now. "Eat first," Haendl said, and took Tropile to a bright and busy sort of food stall. Only it wasn't a stall. It was a restaurant.

This Haendl—what to make of him? He should have been disgusting, nasty, an abomination. He had no manners whatever. He didn't know, or at least didn't use, the Seventeen Conventional Gestures. He wouldn't let Tropile walk behind him and to his left, though he was easily five years Tropile's senior. When he ate, he *ate*. The Sip of Appreciation, the Pause of First Surfeit, the Thrice Proffered Share meant nothing to him. He laughed when Tropile tried to give him the Elder's Portion.

Cheerfully patronizing, this man Haendl said to Tropile: "That stuffs all right when you don't have anything better to do with your time. Those poor mutts don't. They'd die of boredom without their inky-pinky cults and they don't have the resources to do anything bigger. Yes, I do know the Gestures. Seventeen delicate ways of communicating emotions too refined for words. The hell with them, Tropile. I've got words. You'll learn them, too."

Tropile ate silently, trying to think.

A man arrived, threw himself in a chair, glanced curiously at Tropile and said: "Haendl, the Somerville Road. The creek backed up when it froze. Flooded bad. Ruined everything."

Tropile ventured: "The flood ruined the road?"

"The road? No. Say, you must be the fellow Haendl went after. Tropile, that the name?" He leaned across the table, pumped Tropile's hand. "We had the road nicely blocked," he explained. "The flood washed it clean. Now we have to block it again."

Haendl said: "Take the tractor if you need it."

The man nodded and left.

Haendl said: "Eat up. We're wasting time. About that road—we keep all entrances blocked up, see? Why let a lot of sheep in and out?"

"Sheep?"

"The opposite," said Haendl, "of Wolves."

* * * *

Take ten billion people and say that, out of every million of them, one—just one—is different. He has a talent for survival; call him Wolf. Ten thousand of him in a world of ten billion.

Squeeze them, freeze them, cut them down. Let old Rejoice in Messias loom in the terrifying sky and so abduct the Earth that the human race is decimated, fractionated, reduced to what is in comparison a bare handful of chilled, stunned survivors. There aren't ten billion people in the world any more. No, not by a factor of a thousand. Maybe there are as many as ten million, more or less, rattling around in the space their enormous Elder Generations made for them.

And of these ten million, how many are Wolf?

Ten thousand.

"You understand, Tropile?" said Haendl. "We survive. I don't care what you call us. The sheep call us Wolves. Me, I kind of call us Supermen. We have a talent for survival."

Tropile nodded, beginning to understand. "The way I survived the House of the Five Regulations."

Haendl gave him a pitying look. "The way you survived thirty years of Sheephood before that. Come on."

It was a tour of inspection. They went into a building, big, looking like any other big and useful building of the ancients, gray stone walls, windows with ragged spears of glass. Inside, though, it wasn't like the others. Two sub-basements down, Tropile winced and turned away from the flood of violet light that poured out of a quartz bull's-eye on top of a squat steel cone.

"Perfectly harmless, Tropile—you don't have to worry," Haendl boomed. "Know what you're looking at? There's a fusion reactor down there. Heat. Power. All the power we need. Do you know what that means?"

He stared soberly down at the flaring violet light of the inspection port.

"Come on," he said abruptly to Tropile.

Another building, also big, also gray stone. A cracked inscription over the entrance read: ORIAL HALL OF HUMANITIES. The sense-shock this time was not light; it was sound. Hammering, screeching, rattling, rumbling. Men were doing noisy things with metal and machines.

"Repair shop!" Haendl yelled. "See those machines? They belong to our man Innison. We've salvaged them from every big factory ruin we could find. Give Innison a piece of metal—any alloy, any shape—and one of those machines will change it into any other shape and damned near any other alloy. Drill it, cut it, plane it, weld it, smelt it, zone-melt it, bond it—you tell him what to do and he'll do it.

"We got the parts to make six tractors and forty-one cars out of this shop. And we've got other shops—aircraft in Farmingdale and Wichita, armaments in Wilmington. Not that we can't make some armaments here. Innison could build you a tank if he had to, complete with 105-millimeter gun."

"What's a tank?" Tropile asked.

Haendl only looked at him and said: "Come on!"

* * * *

Glenn Tropile's head spun dizzily and all the spectacles merged and danced in his mind. They were incredible. All of them.

Fusion pile, machine shop, vehicular garage, aircraft hangar. There was a storeroom under the seats of a football stadium, and Tropile's head spun on his shoulders again as he tried to count the cases of coffee and canned soups and whiskey and beans. There was another storeroom, only this one was called an armory. It was filled with...guns. Guns that could be loaded with cartridges, of which they had very many; guns which, when you loaded them and pulled the trigger, would fire.

Tropile said, remembering: "I saw a gun once that still had its firing pin. But it was rusted solid."

"These work, Tropile," said Haendl. "You can kill a man with them. Some of us have."

"*Kill*—"

"Get that sheep look out of your eyes, Tropile! What's the difference how you execute a criminal? And what's a criminal but someone who represents a danger to your world? We prefer a gun instead of the Donation of the Spinal Tap, because it's quicker, because it's less messy—and because we don't like to drink spinal fluid, no matter what imaginary therapeutic or symbolic value it has. You'll learn."

But he didn't add "come on." They had arrived where they were going.

It was a small room in the building that housed the armory and it held, among other things, a rack of guns.

"Sit down," said Haendl, taking one of the guns out of the rack thoughtfully and handling it as the doomed Boyne had caressed his watch-case. It was the latest pre-Pyramid-model rifle, anti-personnel, short-range. It would not scatter a cluster of shots in a coffee can at more than two and a half miles.

"All right," said Haendl, stroking the stock. "You've seen the works, Tropile. You've lived thirty years with sheep. You've seen what they have and what we have. I don't have to ask you to make a choice. I know what you choose. The only thing left is to tell you what *we* want from *you*."

A faint pulsing began inside Glenn Tropile. "I expected we'd be getting to that."

"Why not? We're not sheep. We don't act that way. Quid pro quo. Remember that—it saves time. You've seen the quid. Now we come to the quo." He leaned forward. "Tropile, what do you know about the Pyramids?"

"Nothing."

Haendl nodded. "Right. They're all around us and our lives are beggared because of them. And we don't even know why. We don't have the least idea of what they are. Did you know that one of the sheep was Translated in Wheeling when you left?"

"Translated?"

Tropile listened with his mouth open while Haendl told him about what had happened to Citizen Boyne.

"So he didn't make the Donation after all," Tropile said.

"Might have been better if he had," said Haendl. "Still, it gave you a chance to get away. We had heard—never mind how just yet—that Wheeling'd caught itself a Wolf, so we came looking for you. But you were already gone."

* * * *

Tropile said, faintly annoyed: "You were damn near too late."

"Oh, no, Tropile," Haendl assured him. "We're never too late. If you don't have enough guts and ingenuity to get away from sheep, you're no wolf—simple as that. But there's this Translation. We know it happens, but we don't even know what it is. All we know, people disappear. There's a new sun in the sky every five years or so. Who makes it? The Pyramids. How? We don't know that. Sometimes something floats around in the air and we call it an Eye. It has something to do with Translation, something to do with the Pyramids. What? We don't know that."

"We don't know much of anything," interrupted Tropile, trying to hurry him along.

"Not about the Pyramids, no." Haendl shook his head. "Hardly anyone has ever seen one, for that matter."

"Hardly—You mean you have?"

"Oh, yes. There's a Pyramid on Mount Everest, you know. That's not just a story. It's true. I've been there, and it's there. At least, it was there five years ago, right after the last Sun Re-creation. I guess it hasn't moved. It just sits there."

Tropile listened, marveling. To have seen a real Pyramid! Almost he had thought of them as legends, contrived to account for such established physical facts as the Eyes and Translation, as children with a Santa Claus. But this incredible man had seen it!

"Somebody dropped an H-bomb on it, way back," Haendl continued, "and the only thing that happened is that now the North Col is a crater. You can't move the Pyramid. You can't hurt it. But it's alive. It has been there, alive, for a couple of hundred years; and that's about all we know about the Pyramids. Right?"

"Right."

Haendl stood up. "Tropile, that's what all of this is all about!" He gestured around him. "Guns, tanks, airplanes—we want to know more! We're going to find out more and then we're going to fight."

There was a jarring note and Tropile caught at it, sniffing the air. Somehow—perhaps it was his sub-adrenals that told him—this very positive, very self-willed man was just the slightest bit unsure of himself. But Haendl swept on and Tropile, for a moment, forgot to be alert.

"We had a party up Mount Everest five years ago," Haendl was saying. "We didn't find out a thing. Five years before that, and five years before *that*—every time there's a sun, while it is still warm enough to give a party a chance to climb up the sides—we send a team up there. It's a rough job. We give it to the new boys, Tropile. Like you."

There it was. He was being invited to attack a Pyramid.

Tropile hesitated, delicately balanced, trying to get the *feel* of this negotiation. This was Wolf against Wolf; it was hard. There had to be an advantage—

"There is an advantage," Haendl said aloud.

Tropile jumped, but then he remembered: Wolf against Wolf.

Haendl went on: "What you get out of it is your life, in the first place. You understand you can't get out now. We don't want sheep meddling around. And in the second place, there's a considerable hope of gain." He stared at Tropile with a dreamer's eyes. "We don't send parties up there for nothing, you know. We want to get something out of it. What we want is the Earth."

"The Earth?" It reeked of madness. But this man wasn't mad.

"Some day, Tropile, it's going to be us against them. Never mind the sheep—they don't count. It's going to be Pyramids and Wolves, and the Pyramids won't win. And then—"

It was enough to curdle the blood. This man was proposing to *fight*, and against the invulnerable, the godlike Pyramids.

But he was glowing and the fever was contagious. Tropile felt his own blood begin to pound. Haendl hadn't finished his "and then—" but he didn't have to. The "and then" was obvious: And then the world takes up again from the day the wandering planet first came into view. And then we go back to our own solar system and an end to the five-year cycle of frost and hunger.

And then the Wolves can rule a world worth ruling.

It was a meretricious appeal, perhaps, but it could not be refused. Tropile was lost.

He said: "You can put away the gun, Haendl. You've signed me up."

CHAPTER VII

The way to Mount Everest, Tropile glumly found, lay through supervising the colony's nursery school. It wasn't what he had expected, but it had the advantages that while his charges were learning, he was learning, too.

One jump ahead of the three-year-olds, he found that the "wolves," far from being predators on the "sheep," existed with them in a far more complicated ecological relationship. There were Wolves all through sheepdom; they leavened the dough of society.

In barbarously simple prose, a primer said: "The Sons of the Wolf are good at numbers and money. You and your friends play money games almost as soon as you can talk, and you can think in percentages and compound interest when you want to. Most people are not able to do this."

True, thought Tropile subvocally, reading aloud to the tots. That was how it had been with him.

"Sheep are afraid of the Sons of the Wolf. Those of us who live among them are in constant danger of detection and death—although ordinarily a Wolf can take care of himself against any number of sheep." True, too.

"It is one of the most dangerous assignments a Wolf can be given to live among the sheep. Yet it is essential. Without us, they would die—of stagnation, of rot, eventually of hunger."

It didn't have to be spelled out any further. Sheep can't mend their own fences.

The prose was horrifyingly bald and the children were horrifyingly—he choked on the word, but managed to form it in his mind—*competitive*. The verbal taboos lingered, he found, after he had broken through the barriers of behavior.

But it was distressing, in a way. At an age when future Citizens would have been learning their Little Pitcher Ways, these children were learning to fight. The perennial argument about who would get to be Big Bill Zeckendorf when they played a strange game called "Zeckendorf and Hilton" sometimes ended in bloody noses.

And nobody—nobody at all—meditated on Connectivity.

Tropile was warned not to do it himself. Haendl said grimly: "We don't understand it and we don't like what we don't understand. We're suspicious animals, Tropile. As the children grow older, we give them just enough practice so they can go into one meditation and get the feel of it—or pretend to, at any rate. If they have to pass as Citizens, they'll need that much. But more than that we do not allow."

"Allow?" Somehow the word grated; somehow his sub-adrenals began to pulse.

"*Allow!* We have our suspicions and we know for a fact that sometimes people disappear when they meditate. We don't want to disappear. We think it's not a good thing to disappear. Don't meditate, Tropile. You hear?"

* * * *

But later, Tropile had to argue the point. He picked a time when Haendl was free, or as nearly free as that man ever was. The whole adult colony had been out on what they used as a parade ground—it had once been a football field, Haendl said. They had done their regular twice-a-week in-fantry drill, that being one of the prices one paid for living among the free, progressive Wolves instead of the dull and tepid sheep.

Tropile was mightily winded, but he cast himself on the ground near Haendl, caught his breath and said: "Haendl—about meditation."

"What about it?"

"Well, perhaps you don't really grasp it."

Tropile searched for words. He knew what he wanted to say. How could anything that felt as good as Oneness be bad? And wasn't Translation, after all, so rare as hardly to matter? But he wasn't sure he could get through to Haendl in those terms.

He tried: "When you meditate successfully, Haendl, you're one with the Universe. Do you know what I mean? There's no feeling like it. It's indescribable peace, beauty, harmony, repose."

"It's the world's cheapest narcotic," Haendl snorted.

"Oh, now, really—"

"*And* the world's cheapest religion. The stone-broke mutts can't afford gilded idols, so they use their own navels. That's all it is. They can't afford alcohol; they can't even afford the muscular exertion of deep breathing that would throw them into a state of hyperventilated oxygen drunkenness. Then what's left? Self-hypnosis. Nothing else. It's all they can do, so they learn it, they define it as pleasant and good, and they're all fixed up."

Tropile sighed. The man was so stubborn! Then a thought occurred to him and he pushed himself up on his elbows. "Aren't you leaving some-thing out? What about Translation?"

Haendl glowered at him. "That's the part we don't understand."

"But surely self-hypnosis doesn't account for—"

"Surely it doesn't!" Haendl mimicked savagely. "All right. We don't understand it and we're afraid of it. Kindly do not tell me Translation is the supreme act of Un-willing, Total Disavowal of Duality, Unison with the

Brahm-Ground or any such slop. You don't know what it is and neither do we." He started to get up. "All we know is, people vanish. And we want no part of it, so we don't meditate. None of us—including you!"

* * * *

It was foolishness, this close-order drill. Could you defeat the unreachable Himalayan Pyramid with a squads-right flanking maneuver?

And yet it wasn't all foolishness. Close-order drill and 2500-calorie-a-day diet began to put fat and flesh and muscle on Tropile's body, and something other than that on his mind. He had not lost the edge of his acquisitiveness, his drive—his whatever it was that made the difference between Wolf and sheep.

But he had gained something. Happiness? Well, if "happiness" is a sense of purpose, and a hope that the purpose can be accomplished, then happiness. It was a feeling that had never existed in his life before. Always it had been the glandular compulsion to gain an advantage, and that was gone, or anyway almost gone, because it was permitted in the society in which he now lived.

Glenn Tropile sang as he putt-putted in his tractor, plowing the thawing Jersey fields. Still, a faint doubt remained. Squads right against the Pyramids?

Stiffly, Tropile stopped the tractor, slowed the diesel to a steady *thrum* and got off. It was hot—being midsummer of the five-year calendar the Pyramids had imposed. It was time for rest and maybe something to eat.

He sat in the shade of a tree, as farmers always have done, and opened his sandwiches. He was only a mile or so from Princeton, but he might as well have been in Limbo; there was no sign of any living human but himself. The northering sheep didn't come near Princeton—it "happened" that way, on purpose.

He caught a glimpse of something moving, but when he stood up for a better look into the woods on the other side of the field, it was gone. Wolf? *Real* Wolf, that is? It could have been a bear, for that matter—there was talk of wolves and bears around Princeton; and although Tropile knew that much of the talk was assiduously encouraged by men like Haendl, he also knew that some of it was true.

As long as he was up, he gathered straw from the litter of last "year's" head-high grass, gathered sticks under the trees, built a small fire and put water on to boil for coffee. Then he sat back and ate his sandwiches, thinking.

Maybe it was a promotion, going from the nursery school to labor in the fields. Or maybe it wasn't. Haendl had promised him a place in the expedition that would—maybe—discover something new and great and helpful about the Pyramids. And that might still come to pass, because the expedition was far from ready to leave.

Tropile munched his sandwiches thoughtfully. Now *why* was the expedition so far from ready to leave? It was absolutely essential to get there in the warmest weather possible—otherwise Mt. Everest was unclimbable. Generations of alpinists had proved that. That warmest weather was rapidly going by.

And *why* were Haendl and the Wolf colony so insistent on building tanks, arming themselves with rifles, organizing in companies and squads? The H-bomb hadn't flustered the Pyramid. What lesser weapon could?

Uneasily, Tropile put a few more sticks on the fire, staring thoughtfully into the canteen cup of water. It was a satisfyingly hot fire, he noticed abstractedly. The water was very nearly ready to boil.

* * * *

Half across the world, the Pyramid in the Himalays felt, or heard, or tasted—a difference.

Possibly the h-f pulses that had gone endlessly wheep, wheep, wheep were now going wheep-*beep*, wheep-*beep*. Possibly the electromagnetic "taste" of lower-than-red was now spiced with a tang of beyond-violet. Whatever the sign was, the Pyramid recognized it.

A part of the crop it tended was ready to harvest.

The ripening bud had a name, of course, but names didn't matter to the Pyramid. The man named Tropile didn't know he was ripening, either. All that Tropile knew was that, for the first time in nearly a year, he had succeeded in catching each stage of the nine perfect states of water-coming-to-a-boil in its purest form.

It was like...like...well, it was like nothing that anyone but a Water Watcher could understand. He observed. He appreciated. He encompassed and absorbed the myriad subtle perfections of time, of shifting transparency, of sound, of distribution of ebulliency, of the faint, faint odor of steam.

Complete, Glenn Tropile relaxed all his limbs and let his chin rest on his breast-bone.

It was, he thought with placid, crystalline perception, a rare and perfect opportunity for meditation. He thought of Connectivity. (Overhead, a shifting glassy flaw appeared in the thin, still air.) There wasn't any thought of Eyes in the erased palimpsest that was Glenn Tropile's mind. There wasn't any thought of Pyramids or of Wolves. The plowed field before him didn't exist. Even the water, merrily bubbling itself dry, was gone from his perception.

He was beginning to meditate.

Time passed—or stood still—for Tropile; there was no difference. There was no time. He found himself almost on the brink of Understanding.

Something snapped. An intruding blue-bottle drone, maybe, or a twitching muscle. Partly, Tropile came back to reality. Almost, he glanced upward. Almost, he saw the Eye....

It didn't matter. The thing that really mattered, the only thing in the world, was all within his mind; and he was ready, he knew, to find it.

Once more! Try harder!

He let the mind-clearing unanswerable question drift into his mind:

If the sound of two hands together is a clapping, what is the sound of one hand?

Gently he pawed at the question, the symbol of the futility of mind—and therefore the gateway to meditation. Unawareness of self was stealing deliciously over him.

He was Glenn Tropile. He was more than that. He was the water boiling...and the boiling water was he. He was the gentle warmth of the fire, which was—which was, yes, itself the arc of the sky. As each thing was each other thing; water was fire, and fire air; Tropile was the first simmering bubble and the full roll of Well-aged Water was Self, was—more than Self—was—

The answer to the unanswerable question was coming clearer and softer to him. And then, all at once, but not suddenly, for there was no time, it was not close—it *was*.

The answer was his, was him. The arc of sky was the answer, and the answer belonged to sky—to warmth, to all warmths that there are, and to all waters, and—and the answer was—was—

Tropile vanished. The mild thunderclap that followed made the flames dance and the column of steam fray; and then the fire was steady again, and so was the rising steam. But Tropile was gone.

CHAPTER VIII

Haendl plodded angrily through the high grass toward the dull throb of the diesel.

Maybe it had been a mistake to take this Glenn Tropile into the colony. He was more Citizen than Wolf—no, cancel that, Haendl thought; he was more Wolf than Citizen. But the Wolf in him was tainted with sheep's blood. He *competed* like a Wolf, but in spite of everything, he refused to give up some of his sheep's ways. Meditation. He had been cautioned against that. But had he given it up?

He had not.

If it had been entirely up to Haendl, Glenn Tropile would have found himself back among the sheep or dead. Fortunately for Tropile, it was not entirely up to Haendl. The community of Wolves was by no means a democracy, but the leader had a certain responsibility to his constituents, and the responsibility was this: He couldn't afford to be wrong. Like the Old Gray Wolf who protected Mowgli, he had to defend his actions against attack; if he failed to defend, the pack would pull him down.

And Innison thought they needed Tropile—not in spite of the taint of the Citizen that he bore, but because of it.

Haendl bawled: "Tropile! Tropile, where are you?" There was only the wind and the *thrum* of the diesel. It was enormously irritating. Haendl had other things to do than to chase after Glenn Tropile. And where was he? There was the diesel, idling wastefully; there the end of the patterned furrows Tropile had plowed. There a small fire, burning—

And there was Tropile.

Haendl stopped, frozen, his mouth opened, about to yell Tropile's name.

It was Tropile, all right, staring with concentrated, oyster-eyed gaze at the fire and the little pot of water it boiled. Staring. Meditating. And over his head, like flawed glass in a pane, was the thing Haendl feared most of all things on Earth. It was an Eye.

Tropile was on the very verge of being Translated...whatever that was.

Time, maybe, to find out *what* that was! Haendl ducked back into the shelter of the high grass, knelt, plucked his radio communicator from his pocket, urgently called.

"Innison! Innison, will somebody, for God's sake, put Innison on!"

Seconds passed. Voices answered. Then there was Innison.

"Innison, listen! You wanted to catch Tropile in the act of Meditation? All right, you've got him. The old wheat field, south end, under the elms around the creek. Get here fast, Innison—there's an Eye forming above him!"

Luck! Lucky that they were ready for this, and only by luck, because it was the helicopter that Innison had patiently assembled for the attack on Everest that was ready now, loaded with instruments, planned to weigh and measure the aura around the Pyramid—now at hand when they needed it.

That was luck, but there was driving hurry involved, too; it was only a matter of minutes before Haendl heard the wobbling drone of the copter, saw the vanes fluttering low over the hedges, dropping to earth behind the elms.

Haendl raised himself cautiously and peered. Yes, Tropile was still there, and the Eye still above him! But the noise of the helicopter had frayed the spell. Tropile stirred. The Eye wavered and shook—

But did not vanish.

Thanking what passed for his God, Haendl scuttled circuitously around the elms and joined Innison at the copter. Innison was furiously closing switches and pointing lenses.

They saw Tropile sitting there, the Eye growing larger and closer over his head. They had time—plenty of time; oh, nearly a minute of time. They brought to bear on the silent and unknowing form of Glenn Tropile every instrument that the copter carried. They were waiting for Tropile to disappear—

He did.

* * * *

Innison and Haendl hunched at the thunderclap as air rushed in to replace him.

"We've got what you wanted," Haendl said harshly. "Let's read some instruments."

Throughout the Translation, high-tensile magnetic tape on a madly spinning drum had been hurtling under twenty-four recording heads at a hundred feet a second. Output to the recording heads had been from every kind of measuring device they had been able to conceive and build, all loaded on the helicopter for use on Mount Everest—all now pointed directly at Glenn Tropile.

They had, for the instant of Translation, readings from one microsecond to the next on the varying electric, gravitational, magnetic, radiant and molecular-state conditions in his vicinity.

They got back to Innison's workshop, and the laboratory inside it, in less than a minute; but it took hours of playing back the magnetic pulses into machines that turned them into scribed curves on coordinate paper before Innison had anything resembling an answer.

He said: "No mystery. I mean no mystery except the speed. Want to know what happened to Tropile?"

"I do," said Haendl.

"A pencil of electrostatic force maintained by a pinch effect bounced down the approximate azimuth of Everest—God knows how they handled the elevation—and charged him and the area positive. A *big* charge, clear off the scale. They parted company. He was bounced straight up. A meter off the ground, a correcting vector was applied. When last seen, he was headed fast in the direction of the Pyramids' binary—fast! So fast that I would guess he'll get there alive. It takes an appreciable time, a good part of a second, for his protein to coagulate enough to make him sick and then kill him. If the Pyramids strip the charges off him immediately on arrival, as I should think they will, he'll live."

"Friction—"

"Be damned to friction," Innison said calmly. "He carried a packet of air with him and there *was* no friction. How? I don't know. How are they going to keep him alive in space, without the charges that hold air? I don't know. If they don't maintain the charges, can they beat the speed of light? I don't know. I can tell you *what* happened. I can't tell you *how*."

Haendl stood up thoughtfully. "It's something," he said grudgingly.

"It's more than we've ever had—a complete reading at the instant of Translation!"

"We'll get more," Haendl promised. "Innison, now that you know what to look for, go on looking for it. Keep every possible detection device monitored twenty-four hours a day. Turn on everything you've got that'll find a sign of imposed modulation. At any sign—or at anybody's hunch that there *might* be a sign—I'm to be called. If I'm eating. If I'm sleeping. If I'm enjoying with a woman. Call me, you hear? Maybe you were right about Tropile; maybe he did have some use. He might give the Pyramids a bellyache."

Innison, flipping the magnetic tape drum to rewind, said thoughtfully: "It's too bad they've got him. We could have used some more readings."

"Too bad?" Haendl laughed sharply. "This time they've got themselves a Wolf."

* * * *

The Pyramids did have a Wolf—a fact which did not matter in the least to them.

It is not possible to know what "mattered" to a Pyramid except by inference. But it is possible to know that they had no way of telling Wolf from Citizen.

The planet which was their home—Earth's old Moon—was small, dark, atmosphereless and waterless. It was completely built over, much of it with its propulsion devices.

In the old days, when technology had followed war, luxury, government and leisure, the Pyramids' sun had run out of steam; and at about the same time, they had run out of the Components they imported from a neighboring planet. They used the last of their Components to implement their stolid metaphysic of hauling and pushing. They pushed their planet.

They knew where to push it.

Each Pyramid as it stood was a radio-astronomy observatory, powerful and accurate beyond the wildest dreams of Earthly radio-astronomers. From this start, they built instruments to aid their naked senses. They went into a kind of hibernation, reducing their activity to a bare trickle except for a small "crew" and headed for Earth. They had every reason to believe they would find more Components there, and they did.

Tropile was one of them. The only thing which set him apart from the others was that he was the most recent to be stockpiled.

The religion, or vice, or philosophy he practiced made it possible for him to be a Component. Meditation derived from Zen Buddhism was a windfall for the Pyramids, though, of course, they had no idea at all of what lay behind it and did not "care." They knew only that, at certain times, certain potential Components became Components which were no longer merely potential—which were, in fact, ripe for harvesting.

It was useful to them that the minds they cropped were utterly blank. It saved the trouble of blanking them.

Tropile had been harvested at the moment his inhibiting conscious mind had been cleared, for the Pyramids were not interested in him as an entity capable of will and conception. They used only the raw capacity of the human brain and its perceptors.

They used Rashevsky's Number, the gigantic, far more than astronomical expression that denoted the number of switching operations performable within the human brain. They used "subception," the phenomenon by which the reasoning mind, uninhibited by consciousness, reacts directly to stimuli—shortcutting the cerebral censor, avoiding the weighing of shall-I-or-shan't-I that precedes every conscious act.

The harvested minds were—Components.

It is not desirable that your bedroom wall switch have a mind of its own; if you turn the lights on, you want them *on*. So it was with the Pyramids.

A Component was needed in the industrial complex which transformed catabolism products into anabolism products.

* * * *

With long experience gained since their planetfall, Pyramids received the *tabula rasa* that was Glenn Tropile. He arrived in one piece, wearing a blanket of air. Quick-frozen mentally at the moment of inert blankness his Meditation had granted him—the psychic drunkard's coma—he was cushioned on repellent charges as he plummeted down, and instantly stripped of surplus electrostatic charge.

At this point, he was still human; only asleep.

He remained "asleep." Annular fields they used for lifting and lowering seized him and moved him into a snug tank of nutrient fluid. There were many such tanks, ready and waiting.

The tanks themselves could be moved, and the one containing Glenn Tropile did move, to a metabolism complex where there were many other tanks, all occupied. This was a warm room—the Pyramids had wasted no energy on such foppish comforts in the first "room." In this room, Glenn Tropile gradually resumed the appearance of life. His heart once again began to beat. Faint stirrings were visible in his chest as his habit-numbed lungs attempted to breathe. Gradually the stirrings slowed and stopped. There was no need for that foppish comfort, either; the nutrient fluid supplied all.

Tropile was "wired into circuit."

The only literal wiring, at first, was a temporary one—a fine electrode aseptically introduced into the great nerve that leads to the rhinencephalon—the "small brain," the area of the brain which contains the pleasure centers that motivate human behavior.

More than a thousand Components had been spoiled and discarded before the Pyramids had located the pleasure centers so exactly.

While the Component, Tropile, was being "programmed," the wire rewarded him with minute pulses that made his body glow with animal satisfaction when he functioned correctly. That was all there was to it. After a time, the wire was withdrawn, but by then Tropile had "learned" his entire task. Conditioned reflexes had been established. They could be counted on for the long and useful life of the Component.

That life might be very long indeed; in the nutrient tank beside Tropile's, as it happened, lay a Component with eight legs and a chitinous fringe around its eyes. It had lain in such a tank for more than a hundred and twenty-five thousand Terrestrial years.

* * * *

The Component was placed in operation. It opened its eyes and saw things. The sensory nerves of its limbs felt things. The muscles of its hands and toes operated things.

Where was Glenn Tropile?

He was there, all of him, but a zombie-Tropile. Bereft of will, emptied of memories. He was a machine and part of a huger machine. His sex was the sex of a photoelectric cell; his politics were those of a transistor; his ambition that of a mercury switch. He didn't know anything about sex, or fear, or hope. He only knew two things: Input and Output.

Input to him was a display of small lights on a board before his vacant face; and also the modulation of a loudspeaker's liquid-borne hum in each ear.

Output from him was the dancing manipulation of certain buttons and keys, prompted by changes in Input and by nothing else.

Between Input and Output, he lay in the tank, a human Black Box which was capable of Rashevsky's Number of switchings, and of nothing else.

He had been programmed to accomplish a specific task—to shepherd a chemical called 3, 7, 12-trihydroxycholanic acid, present in the catabolic product of the Pyramids, through a succession of more than five hundred separate operations until it emerged as the chemical, which the Pyramids were able to metabolize, called Protoporphin IX.

He was not the only Component operating in this task; there were several, each with its own program.

The acid accumulated in great tanks a mile from him. He knew its concentration, heat and pressure; he knew of all the impurities which would affect subsequent reactions. His fingers tapped, giving binary-coded signals to sluice gates to open for so many seconds and then to close; for such an amount of solvent at such a temperature to flow in; for the agitators to agitate for just so long at just such a force. And if a trouble signal disturbed any one of the 517 major and minor operations, he—it?—was set to decide among alternatives:

—scrap the batch in view of flow conditions along the line?

—isolate and bypass the batch through a standby loop?

—immediate action to correct the malfunction?

Without inhibiting intelligence, without the trammels of humanity on him, the intricate display board and the complex modulations of the two sound signals could be instantly taken in, evaluated and given their share in the decision.

Was it—he?—still alive?

The question has no meaning. It was working. It was an excellent machine, in fact, and the Pyramids cared for it well. Its only consciousness, apart from the reflexive responses that were its program, was—well, call it "the sound of one hand alone." Which is to say zero, mindlessness, Samadhi, stupor.

It continued to function for some time—until the required supply of Protoporphin IX had been exceeded by a sufficient factor of safety to make further processing unnecessary—that is, for some minutes or months. During that time, it was Happy. (It had been programmed to be Happy when there were no uncorrected malfunctions of the process.) At the end of that time, it shut itself off, sent out a signal that the task was completed, then it was laid aside in the analogue of a deep-freeze, to be reprogrammed when another Component was needed.

It was totally immaterial to the Pyramids that this particular Component had not been stamped from Citizen but from Wolf.

CHAPTER IX

Roget Germyn, of Wheeling a Citizen, contemplated his wife with growing concern.

Possibly the events of the past few days had unhinged her reason, but he was nearly sure that she had eaten a portion of the evening meal secretly, in the serving room, before calling him to the table.

He felt positive that it was only a temporary aberration; she was, after all, a Citizeness, with all that that implied. A—a creature—like that Gala Tropile, for example—someone like that might steal extra portions with craft and guile. You couldn't live with a Wolf for years and not have some of it rub off on you. But not Citizeness Germyn.

There was a light, thrice-repeated tap on the door.

Speak of the devil, thought Roget Germyn most appropriately; for it was that same Gala Tropile. She entered, her head downcast, looking worn and—well, pretty.

He began formally: "I give you greeting, Citi—"

"They're here!" she interrupted in desperate haste. Germyn blinked. "Please," she begged, "can't you do something? They're *Wolves*!"

Citizeness Germyn emitted a muted shriek.

"You may leave, Citizeness," Germyn told her shortly, already forming in his mind the words of gentle reproof he would later use. "Now what is all this talk of Wolves?"

Gala Tropile distractedly sat in the chair her hostess had vacated. "We were running away," she babbled. "Glenn—he was Wolf, you see, and he made me leave with him, after the House of the Five Regulations. We were a day's long march from Wheeling and we stopped to rest. And there was an aircraft, Citizen!"

"An aircraft!" Citizen Germyn allowed himself a frown. "Citizeness, it is not well to invent things which are not so."

"I saw it, Citizen! There were men in it. One of them is here again! He came looking for me with another man and I barely escaped him. I'm afraid!"

"There is no cause for fear, only an opportunity to appreciate," Citizen Germyn said mechanically—it was what one told one's children.

But within himself, he was finding it very hard to remain calm. That word Wolf—it was a destroyer of calm, an incitement to panic and hatred! He remembered Tropile well, and there was Wolf, to be sure. The mere fact that Citizen Germyn had doubted his Wolfishness at first was powerful cause to be doubly convinced of it now; he had postponed the day of reckoning for an enemy of all the world, and there was enough secret guilt in his recollection to set his own heart thumping.

"Tell me exactly what happened," said Citizen Germyn, in words that the stress of emotion had already made far less than graceful.

Obediently, Gala Tropile said: "I was returning to my home after the evening meal and Citizeness Puffin—she took me in after Citizen Tropile—after my husband was—"

"I understand. You made your home with her."

"Yes. She told me that two men had come to see me. They spoke badly, she said, and I was alarmed. I peered through a window of my home and they were there. One had been in the aircraft I saw! And they flew away with my husband."

"It is a matter of seriousness," Citizen Germyn admitted doubtfully. "So then you came here to me?"

"Yes, but they saw me, Citizen! And I think they followed. You must protect me—I have no one else!"

"If they be Wolf," Germyn said calmly, "we will raise hue and cry against them. Now will the Citizeness remain here? I go forth to see these men."

There was a graceless hammering on the door.

"Too late!" cried Gala Tropile in panic. "They are here!"

* * * *

Citizen Germyn went through the ritual of greeting, of deprecating the ugliness and poverty of his home, of offering everything he owned to his visitors; it was the way to greet a stranger.

The two men lacked both courtesy and wit, but they did make an attempt to comply with the minimal formal customs of introduction. He had to give them credit for that; and yet it was almost more alarming than if they had blustered and yelled.

For he knew one of these men.

He dredged the name out of his memory. It was Haendl. The same man had appeared in Wheeling the day Glenn Tropile had been scheduled to make the Donation of the Spinal Tap—and had broken free and escaped. He had inquired about Tropile of a good many people, Citizen Germyn included, and even at that time, in the excitement of an Amok, a Wolf-finding and a Translation in a single day, Germyn had wondered at Haendl's lack of breeding and airs.

Now he wondered no longer.

But the man made no overt act and Citizen Germyn postponed the raising of the hue and cry. It was not a thing to be done lightly.

"Gala Tropile is in this house," the man with Haendl said bluntly.

Citizen Germyn managed a Quirked Smile.

"We want to see her, Germyn. It's about her husband. He—uh—he was with us for a while and something happened."

"Ah, yes. The Wolf."

The man flushed and looked at Haendl. Haendl said loudly: "The Wolf. Sure he's a Wolf. But he's gone now, so you don't have to worry about that."

"Gone?"

"Not just him, but four or five of us. There was a man named Innison and he's gone, too. We need help, Germyn. Something about Tropile—God knows how it is, but he started something. We want to talk to his wife and find out what we can about him. So will you get her out of the back room where she's hiding and bring her here, please?"

Citizen Germyn quivered. He bent over the ID bracelet that once had belonged to the one PFC Joe Hartman, fingering it to hide his thoughts.

He said at last: "Perhaps you are right. Perhaps the Citizeness is with my wife. If this be so, would it not be possible that she is fearful of those who once were with her husband?"

* * * *

Haendl laughed sourly. "She isn't any more fearful than we are, Germyn. I told you about this man Innison who disappeared. He was a Son of the Wolf, you understand me? For that matter—" He glanced at his companion, licked his lips and changed his mind about what he had been going to say next. "He was a Wolf. Do you ever remember hearing of a Wolf being Translated before?"

"Translated?" Germyn dropped the ID bracelet. "But that's impossible!" he cried, forgetting his manners completely. "Oh, no! Translation comes only to those who attain the moment of supreme detachment, you can be sure of that. I *know*! I've seen it with my own eyes. No Wolf could possibly—"

"At least five Wolves did," Haendl said grimly. "Now you see what the trouble is? Tropile was Translated—I saw that with *my* own eyes. The next day, Innison. Within a week, two or three others. So we came down here, Germyn, not because we like you people, not because we enjoy it, but because we're *scared*.

"What we want is to talk to Tropile's wife—you, too, I guess; we want to talk to anybody who ever knew him. We want to find out everything there is to find out about Tropile and see if we can make any sense of the answers. Because maybe Translation is the supreme objective of life to you people, Germyn, but to us it's just one more way of dying. And we don't want to die."

Citizen Germyn bent to pick up his cherished identification bracelet and dropped it absently on a table. There was very much on his mind.

He said at last: "That is strange. Shall I tell you another strange thing?"

Haendl, looking angry and baffled, nodded.

Germyn said: "There has been no Translation here since the day the Wolf, Tropile, escaped. But there have been Eyes. I have seen them myself. It—" He hesitated, shrugged. "It has been disturbing. Some of our finest Citizens have ceased to Meditate; they have been worrying. So many Eyes and nobody taken! It is outside of all of our experience, and our customs have suffered. Politeness is dwindling among us. Even in my own household—"

He coughed and went on: "No matter. But these Eyes have come into every home; they have peered about, peered about, and no one has been taken. Why? Is it something to do with the Translation of Wolves?" He stared hopelessly at his visitors. "All I know is that it is very strange and therefore I am worried."

"Then take us to Gala Tropile," said Haendl. "Let's see what we can find out!"

Citizen Germyn bowed. He cleared his throat and raised his voice just sufficiently to carry from one room to another. "Citizeness!" he called.

There was a pause and then his wife appeared in the doorway, looking ruffled and ill at ease with her guest.

"Will you ask if Citizeness Tropile will join us here?" he requested.

His wife nodded. "She is resting. I will call her."

They called her and questioned her for some time.

She told them nothing.

She had nothing to tell.

CHAPTER X

On Earth's binary, Glenn Tropile had been reprogrammed for a new task.

The problem was navigation. Earth had been a disappointment to the Pyramids; it was necessary to move rapidly to a more rewarding planet.

The Pyramids had taken Earth out past Pluto's orbit with a simple shove, slow and massive. It had been enough merely to approximate the direction in which they would want to go. There would be plenty of time for refinements of course later.

But now the time for refinements had come, earlier than they might have expected. They had now time to travel, they knew where to—a star cluster reasonably sure to be rich in Componentiferous planets. It was inherent in the nature of Component mines that eventually they always played out.

There were always more mines, though. If that had not been so, it would have been necessary, perhaps, to stock-breed Components against future needs. But it was easier to work the vein out and move on.

Now the course had to be computed. There were such variables to be considered as: motion of the star cluster; acceleration of the binary-planet system; *gravitational influence of every astronomical object in the island universe, without exception.*

Precise computation on this basis was obviously not practical. That was not an answer to the problem, since the time required would approach eternity as one of its parameters.

It was possible to simplify the problem. Only the astronomical bodies which were relatively nearby need be treated as individuals. Farther away, the Pyramids began to group them in small bunches, still farther in large bunches, on to the point where the farthest—and the most numerous—bodies were lumped together as a vague gravitational "noise" whose average intensity alone it was required to know and to enter as a datum.

And still no single Component could handle even its own share of the problem, were the "computer" they formed to be kept within the range of permissible size.

It was for this that the Component which had once been Tropile was taken out of storage.

This was all old stuff to the Pyramids; they knew how to handle it. They broke the problem down to its essentials, separated even those into many parts. There was, for example, the subsection of one certain aspect of the logistical problem which involved locating and procuring additional Components to handle the load.

Even that tiny specialization was too much for a single Component, but fortunately the Pyramids had resources to bring to bear. The procedure in such cases was to hitch several Components together.

This was done.

When the Pyramids finished their neuro-surgery, there floated in an oversized nutrient tank a thing like a great sea-anemone. It was composed of eight Components—all human, as it happened—arranged in a circle, facing inward, joined temple to temple, brain to brain.

At their feet, where sixteen eyes could see it, was the display board to feed them their Input. Sixteen hands each grasped a molded switch to handle their binary-coded Output. There would be no storage of the Output outside of the eight-Component complex itself; it went as control signals to the electrostatic generators, funneled through the single Pyramid on Mount Everest, which handled the task of Component-procurement.

That is, of Translation.

The programming was slow and thorough. Perhaps the Pyramid which finally activated the octuple unit and went away was pleased with itself, not knowing that one of its Components was Glenn Tropile.

* * * *

Nirvana. (It pervaded all; there was nothing outside of it.)

Nirvana. (Glenn Tropile floated in it as in the amniotic fluid around him.)

Nirvana. (The sound of one hand.... Floating oneness.)

There was an intrusion.

Perfection is completed; by adding to it, it is destroyed. *Duality struck like a thunderbolt. Oneness shattered.*

For Glenn Tropile, it seemed as though his wife were screaming at him to wake up. He tried to.

It was curiously difficult and painful. Timeless poignant sadness, five years of sorrow over a lost love compressed into a microsecond. It was always so, Tropile thought drowsily, awakening. It never lasts. What's the use of worrying over what always happens....

Sudden shock and horror rocked him.

This was no ordinary awakening—no ordinary thing at all—*nothing* was as it ever had been before!

Tropile opened his mouth and screamed—or thought he did. But there was only a hoarse, faint flutter in his eardrums.

It was a moment when sanity might have gone. But there was one curious, mundane fact that saved him. He was holding something in his hands. He found that he could look at it, and it was a switch. A molded switch, mounted on a board, and he was holding one in each hand.

It was little to cling to, but it at least was real. If his hands could be holding something, then there must be some reality somewhere.

Tropile closed his eyes and managed to open them again. Yes, there was reality, too. He closed his eyes and light stopped. He opened them and light returned.

Then perhaps he was not dead, as he had thought.

Carefully, stumbling—his mind his only usable tool—he tried to make an estimate of his surroundings.

He could hardly believe what he found.

Item: he could scarcely move. Somehow he was bound by his feet and his head. How? He couldn't tell.

Item: he was bent over and he couldn't straighten. Why? Again he couldn't tell, but it was a fact. The great erecting muscles of his back answered his command, but his body would not move.

Item: his eyes saw, but only in a small area.

He couldn't move his head, either. Still, he could see a few things. The switch in his hand, his feet, a sort of display of lights on a strangely circular board.

The lights flickered and changed their pattern.

* * * *

Without thinking, he moved a switch. Why? Because it was *right* to move that switch. When a certain light flared green, a certain switch had to be thrown. Why? Well, when a certain light flared green, a certain switch—

He abandoned that problem. Never mind why; what the devil was going *on*?

Glenn Tropile squinted about him like a mollusc peering out of its shell. There was another fact, the oddness of the seeing. What makes it look so queer, he asked himself.

He found an answer, but it required some time to take it in. He was seeing in a strange perspective. One looks out of two eyes. Close one eye and the world is flat. Open it again and there is a stereoscopic double; the saliencies of the picture leap forward, the background retreats.

So with the lights on the board—no, not exactly; but something *like* that, he thought. It was as though—he squinted and strained—well, as though he had never really *seen* before. As though for all his life he had had only one eye, and now he had strangely been given two.

His visual perception of the board was *total*. He could see all of it at once. It had no "front" or "back." It was in the round. The natural thinking of it was without orientation. He engulfed and comprehended it as a unit. It had no secrets of shadow or silhouette.

I think, Tropile mouthed slowly to himself, that I'm going crazy.

But that was no explanation, either. Mere insanity didn't account for what he saw.

Then, he asked himself, was he in a state that was *beyond* Nirvana? He remembered, with an odd flash of guilt, that he had been Meditating, watching the stages of boiling water. All right, perhaps he had been Translated. But what was this, then? Were the Meditators wrong in teaching that Nirvana was the end—and yet righter than the Wolves, who dismissed Meditation as a phenomenon wholly inside the skull and refused to discuss Translation at all?

That was a question for which he could find nothing approaching an answer. He turned away from it and looked at his hands.

He could see them, too, in the round, he noted. He could see every wrinkle and pore in all sixteen of them....

Sixteen hands!

* * * *

That was the other moment when sanity might have gone. He closed his eyes. (Sixteen eyes! No wonder the total perception!) And, after a while, he opened them again.

The hands were there. All sixteen of them.

Cautiously, Tropile selected a finger that seemed familiar in his memory. After a moment's thought, he flexed it. It bent. He selected another. Another—on a different hand this time.

He could use any or all of the sixteen hands. They were all his, all sixteen of them.

I appear, thought Tropile crazily, to be a sort of eight-branched snowflake. Each of my branches is a human body.

He stirred, and added another datum: I appear also to be in a tank of fluid and yet I do not drown.

There were certain deductions to be made from that. Either someone—the Pyramids?—had done something to his lungs, or else the fluid was as good an oxygenating medium as air. Or both.

Suddenly a burst of data-lights twinkled on the board below him. Instantly and involuntarily, his sixteen hands began working the switches, transmitting complex directions in a lightninglike stream of on-off clicks.

Tropile relaxed and let it happen. He had no choice; the power that made it *right* to respond to the board made it impossible for his brain to concentrate while the response was going on. Perhaps, he thought drowsily, he would never have awakened at all if it had not been for the long period with no lights....

But he was awake. And his consciousness began to explore as the task ended.

He had had an opportunity to understand something of what was happening. He understood that he was now a part of something larger than himself, beyond doubt something which served and belonged to the Pyramids. His single brain not being large enough for the job, seven others had been hooked in with it.

But where were their personalities?

Gone, he supposed; presumably they had been Citizens. Sons of the Wolf did not Meditate and therefore were not Translated—except for himself, he corrected wryly, remembering the Meditation on Rainclouds that had led him to—

No, wait!

Not Rainclouds but Water!

* * * *

Tropile caught hold of himself and forced his mind to retrace that thought. He *remembered* the Raincloud Meditation. It had been prompted by a particularly noble cumulus of the Ancient Ship type.

And this was odd. Tropile had never been deeply interested in Rainclouds, had never known even the secondary classifications of Raincloud types. And he *knew* that the Ancient Ship was of the fourth order of categories.

It was a false memory.

It was not his.

Therefore, logically, it was someone else's memory; and being available to his own mind, as the fourteen other hands and eyes were available, it must belong to—another branch of the snowflake.

He turned his eyes down and tried to see which of the branches was his old body. He found it quickly, with growing excitement. There was the left great toe of his body. He had injured it in boyhood and there was no mistaking the way it was bent. Good! It was reassuring.

He tried to feel the one particular body that led to that familiar toe.

He succeeded, though not easily. After a time, he became more aware of *that* body—somewhat as a neurotic may become "stomach conscious" or "heart conscious." But this was no neurosis; it was an intentional exploration.

Since that worked, with some uneasiness he transferred his attention to another pair of feet and "thought" his way up from them.

It was embarrassing.

For the first time in his life, he knew what it felt like to have breasts. For the first time in his life, he knew what it was like to have one's internal organs quite differently shaped and arranged, buttressed and stressed by different muscles. The very faint background feel of man's internal arrangements, never questioned unless something goes wrong with them and they start to hurt, was not at all like the faint background feel that a woman has inside her.

And when he concentrated on that feel, it was no faint background to him. It was surprising and upsetting.

He withdrew his attention—hoping that he would be able to. Gratefully, he became conscious of his own body again. He was still *himself* if he chose to be.

Were the other seven still themselves?

He reached into his mind—all of it, all eight separate intelligences that were combined within him.

"Is anybody there?" he demanded.

No answer—or nothing he could recognize as an answer. He drove harder and there still was none. It was annoying. He resented it as bitterly, he remembered, as in the old days when he had first been learning the subtleties of Ruin Appreciation. There had been a Ruin Master, his name forgotten, who had been sometimes less than courteous, had driven hard—

Another false memory!

He withdrew and weighed it. Perhaps, he thought, that was a part of the answer. These people, these other seven, would not be driven. The attempt to call them back to consciousness would have to be delicate. When he drove hard, it was painful—he remembered the instant violent agony of his own awakening—and they reacted with anguish.

* * * *

More gently, alert for vagrant "memories," he combed the depths of the eightfold mind within him, reaching into the sleeping portions, touching, handling, sifting and associating, sorting. This memory of an old knife wound from an Amok—that was not the Raincloud woman; it was a man, very aged. This faint recollection of a childhood fear of drowning—was that she? It was; it fitted with this other recollection, the long detour on the road south toward the sun, around a river.

The Raincloud woman was the first to round out in his mind, and the first he communicated with. He was not surprised to find that, early in her life, she had feared that she might be Wolf.

He reached out for her. It was almost magic—knowing the "secret name" of a person, so that then he was yours to command. But the "secret name" was more than that. It was the gestalt of the person. It was the sum of all data and experience, never available to another person—until now.

With her memories arranged at last in his own mind, he thought persuasively: "Citizeness Alla Narova, will you awaken and speak with me?"

No answer—only a vague, troubled stirring.

Gently he persisted: "I know you well, Alla Narova. You sometimes thought you might be a Daughter of the Wolf, but never really believed it because you knew you loved your husband—and thought Wolves did not love. You loved Rainclouds, too. It was when you stood at Beachy Head and saw a great cumulus that you went into Meditation—"

And on and on, many times, coaxingly. Even so, it was not easy; but at last he began to reach her. Slowly she began to surface. Thoughts faintly sounded in his mind, like echoes at first, his own thoughts bouncing back at him, a sort of mental nod of agreement: "Yes, that is so." Then—terror. With a shaking fear, a hysterical rush, Citizeness Alla Narova came violently up to full consciousness and to panic.

She was soundlessly screaming. The whole eight-branched figure quivered and twisted in its nutrient bath.

The terrible storm raged in Tropile's own mind as fully as in hers—but he had the advantage of knowing what it was. He helped her. He fought it for the two of them…soothing, explaining, calming.

At last her branch of the snowflake-body retreated, sobbing for a spell. The storm was over.

He talked to her in his mind and she "listened." She was incredulous, but there was no choice for her; she *had* to believe.

Exhausted and passive, she asked finally: "What can we do? I wish I were dead!"

He told her: "You were never a coward before. Remember, Alla Narova, I *know* you as nobody has ever known another human being before. That's the way you will know me. As for what we can do—we must begin by waking the others, if we can."

"If not?"

"If not," Tropile replied grimly, "then we will think of something else."

She was of tough stuff, he thought admiringly. When she had rested and absorbed things, her spirit was almost that of a Wolf; she had very nearly been right about herself.

Together they explored their twinned members. They found through them exactly what task was theirs to do. They found how the electrostatic harvesting scythe of the Pyramids was controlled, by and through them. They found what limitations there were and what freedoms they owned. They reached into the other petals of the snowflake, reached past the linked

Components into the whole complex of electrostatic field generators and propulsion machinery, reached even past that into—

Into the great single function of the Pyramids that lay beyond.

CHAPTER XI

Haendl was on the ragged edge of breakdown, which was something new in his life.

It was full hot summer and the hidden colony of Wolves in Princeton should have been full of energy and life. The crops were growing on all the fields nearby; the drained storehouses were being replenished.

The aircraft that had been so painfully rebuilt and fitted for the assault on Mount Everest were standing by, ready to be manned and to take off.

And nothing, absolutely nothing, was going right.

It looked as though there would *be* no expedition to Everest. Four times now, Haendl had gathered his forces and been all ready. Four times, a key man of the expedition had—vanished.

Wolves didn't vanish!

And yet more than a score of them had. First Tropile—then Innison—then two dozen more, by ones and twos. No one was immune. Take Innison, for example. There was a man who was Wolf through and through. He was a doer, not a thinker; his skills were the skills of an artisan, a tinkerer, a jackleg mechanic. How could a man like that succumb to the pallid lure of Meditation?

But undeniably he had.

It had reached a point where Haendl himself was red-eyed and jumpy. He had set curious alarms for himself—had enlisted the help of others of the colony to avert the danger of Translation from himself.

When he went to bed at night, a lieutenant sat next to his bed, watchfully alert lest Haendl, in that moment of reverie before sleep, fell into Meditation and himself be Translated. There was no hour of the day when Haendl permitted himself to be alone; and his companions, or guards, were ordered to shake him awake, as violently as need be, at the first hint of an abstracted look in the eyes or a reflective cast of the features.

As time went on, Haendl's self-imposed regime of constant alertness began to cost him heavily in lost rest and sleep. And the consequences of that were—more and more occasions when the bodyguards shook him awake; less and less rest.

He was very close to breakdown indeed.

On a hot, wet morning a few days after his useless expedition to see Citizen Germyn in Wheeling, Haendl ate a tasteless breakfast and, reeling with fatigue, set out on a tour of inspection of Princeton. Warm rain dripped from low clouds, but that was merely one more annoyance to Haendl. He hardly noticed it.

There were upward of a thousand Wolves in the Community and there were signs of worry on the face of every one of them. Haendl was not the only man in Princeton who had begun laying traps for himself as a result of the unprecedented disappearances; he was not the only one who was short of sleep. When one member in forty disappears, the morale of the whole community receives a shattering blow.

To Haendl, it was clear, looking into the faces of his compatriots, that not only was it going to be nearly impossible to mount the planned assault on the Pyramid on Everest this year, it was going to be unbearably difficult merely to keep the community going.

The whole Wolf pack was on the verge of panic.

* * * *

There was a confused shouting behind Haendl. Groggily he turned and looked; half a dozen Wolves were yelling and pointing at something in the wet, muggy air.

It was an Eye, hanging silent and featureless over the center of the street.

Haendl took a deep breath and mustered command of himself. "Frampton!" he ordered one of his lieutenants. "Get the helicopter with the instruments here. We'll take some more readings."

Frampton opened his mouth, then looked more closely at Haendl and, instead, began to talk on his pocket radio. Haendl knew what was in the man's mind—it was in his own, too.

What was the use of more readings? From the time of Tropile's Translation on, they had had a superfluity of instrument readings on the forces and auras that surrounded the Eyes—yes, and on Translations themselves, too. Before Tropile, there had never been an Eye seen in Princeton, much less an actual Translation. But things were different now. Everything was different. Eyes roamed restlessly around day and night.

Some of the men nearest the Eye were picking up rocks and throwing them at the bobbing vortex in the air. Haendl started to yell at them to stop, then changed his mind. The Eye didn't seem to be affected—as he watched, one of the men scored a direct hit with a cobblestone. The stone went right through the Eye, without sound or effect; why not let them work off some of their fears in direct action?

There was a fluttering of vanes and the copter with the instruments mounted on it came down in the middle of the street, between Haendl and the Eye.

It was all very rapid from then on.

The Eye swooped toward Haendl. He couldn't help it; he ducked. That was useless, but it was also unnecessary, for he saw in a second that it was only partly the motion of the Eye toward him that made it loom larger; it was also that the Eye itself was growing.

An Eye was perhaps the size of a football, as near as anyone could judge. This one got bigger, bigger. It was the size of a roc's egg, the size of a whale's blunt head. It stopped and hovered over the helicopter, while the man inside frantically pointed lenses and meters—

Thundercrash.

Not a man this time—Translation had gone beyond men. The whole helicopter vanished, man, instruments, spinning vanes and all.

Haendl picked himself up, sweating, shocked beyond sleepiness.

The young man named Frampton said fearfully: "Haendl, what do we do now?"

"Do?" Haendl stared at him absently. "Why, kill ourselves, I guess."

He nodded soberly, as though he had at last attained the solution of a difficult problem. Then he sighed.

"Well, one thing before that," he said. "I'm going to Wheeling. We Wolves are licked; maybe the Citizens can help us now."

* * * *

Roget Germyn, of Wheeling, a Citizen, received the message in the chambers that served him as a place of business. He had a visitor waiting for him at home.

Germyn was still Citizen and he could not quickly break off the pleasant and interminable discussion he was having with a prospective client over a potential business arrangement. He apologized for the interruption caused by the message the conventional five times, listened while his guest explained once more the plan he had come to propose in full, then turned his cupped hands toward himself in the gesture of Denial of Adequacy. It was the closest he could come to saying no.

On the other side of the desk, the Citizen who had come to propose an investment scheme immediately changed the subject by inviting Germyn and his Citizeness to a Sirius Viewing, the invitation in the form of rhymed couplets. He had wanted to transact his business very much, but he couldn't *insist*.

Germyn got out of the invitation by a Conditional Acceptance in proper form, and the man left, delayed only slightly by the Four Urgings to Stay. Almost immediately, Germyn dismissed his clerk and closed his office for the day by tying a triple knot in a length of red cord across the open door.

When he got to his home, he found, as he had suspected, that the visitor was Haendl.

There was much doubt in Citizen Germyn's mind about Haendl. The man had nearly admitted to being Wolf, and how could a citizen overlook that? But in the excitement of Gala Tropile's Translation, there had been no hue and cry. Germyn had permitted the man to leave. And now?

He reserved judgment. He found Haendl distastefully sipping tea in the living room and attempting to keep up a formal conversation with Citizeness Germyn. He rescued him, took him aside, closed a door—and waited.

He was astonished at the change in the man. Before, Haendl had been bouncy, aggressive, quick-moving—the very qualities least desired in a Citizen, the mark of the Son of the Wolf. Now he was none of these things, but he looked no more like a Citizen for all that; he was haggard, tense.

He said, with an absolute minimum of protocol: "Germyn, the last time I saw you, there was a Translation. Gala Tropile, remember?"

"I remember," Citizen Germyn said. Remember! It had hardly left his thoughts.

"And you told me there had been others. Are they still going on?"

* * * *

Germyn said: "There have been others." He was trying to speak directly, to match this man Haendl's speed and forcefulness. It was hardly good manners, but it had occurred to Citizen Germyn that there were times when manners, after all, were not the most important thing in the world. "There were two in the past few days. One was a woman—Citizeness Baird; her husband's a teacher. She was Viewing Through Glass with four or five other women at the time. She just—disappeared. She was looking through a green prism at the time, if that helps."

"I don't know if it helps or not. Who was the other one?"

Germyn shrugged. "A man named Harmane. No one saw it. But they heard the thunderclap, or something like a thunderclap, and he was missing." He thought for a moment. "It is a little unusual, I suppose. Two in a week—"

Haendl said roughly: "Listen, Germyn. It isn't just two. In the past thirty days, within the area around here and in *one other place*, there have been at least fifty. In *two* places, do you understand? Here and in Princeton. The rest of the world—nothing much; a few Translations here and there. But just in these two communities, fifty. Does that make sense?"

Citizen Germyn thought. "—No."

"No. And I'll tell you something else. Three of the—well, victims have been children under the age of five. One was too young to walk. And the most recent Translation wasn't a person at all. It was a helicopter. Now figure that out, Germyn. What's the explanation for Translations?"

Germyn was gaping. "Why—you Meditate, you know. On Connectivity. The idea is that once you've grasped the Essential Connectivity of All Things, you become One with the Cosmic Whole. But I don't see how a baby or a machine—"

"No, of course you don't. Remember Glenn Tropile?"

"Naturally."

"He's the link," Haendl said grimly. "When he got Translated, we thought it was a big help, because he had the consideration to do it right under our eyes. We got enough readings to give us a clue as to what, physically speaking, Translation is all about. That was the first real clue and we thought he'd done us a favor. Now I'm not so sure."

He leaned forward. "Every person I know of who was Translated was someone Tropile knew. The three kids were in his class at the nursery school—we put him there for a while to keep him busy, when he first came to us. Two of the men he bunked with are gone; the mess boy who served him is gone; his wife is gone. Meditation? No, Germyn. I know most of those people. Not a damned one of them would have spent a moment Meditating on Connectivity to save his life. And what do you make of that?"

* * * *

Swallowing hard, Germyn said: "I just remembered. That man Harmane—"

"What about him?"

"The one who was Translated last week. He also knew Tropile. He was the Keeper of the House of the Five Regulations when Tropile was there."

"You see? And I'll bet the woman knew Tropile, too." Haendl got up fretfully, pacing around. "Here's the thing, Germyn. I'm licked. You know what I am, don't you?"

Germyn said levelly: "I believe you to be Wolf."

"You believe right. That doesn't matter any more. You don't like Wolves. Well, I don't like you. But this thing is too big for me to care about that any more. Tropile has started something happening, and what the end of it is going to be, I can't tell. But I know this: We're not safe, either of us. Maybe you still think Translation is a fulfillment. I don't; it scares me. *But it's going to happen to me*—and to you. It's going to happen to everybody who ever had anything to do with Glenn Tropile, unless we can somehow stop it—and I don't know how. Will you help me?"

Germyn, trying not to tremble when all his buried fears screamed *Wolf!*, said honestly: "I'll have to sleep on it."

Haendl looked at him for a moment. Then he shrugged. Almost to himself, he said: "Maybe it doesn't matter. Maybe we can't do anything about it anyhow. All right. I'll come back in the morning, and if you've made up your mind to help, we'll start trying to make plans. And if you've made up your mind the other way—well, I guess I'll have to fight off a few Citizens. Not that I mind that."

Germyn stood up and bowed. He began the ritual Four Urgings.

"Spare me that," Haendl growled. "Meanwhile, Germyn, if I were you, I wouldn't make any long-range plans. You may not be here to carry them out."

Germyn asked thoughtfully: "And if you were *you*?"

"I'm not making any," Haendl said grimly.

* * * *

Citizen Germyn, feeling utterly tainted with the scent of the Wolf in his home, tossed in his bed, sleepless. His eyes were wide open, staring at the dark ceiling. He could hear his wife's decorous breathing from the foot of the bed—soft and regular, it should have been lulling him to sleep.

It was not. Sleep was very far away.

Germyn was a brave enough man, as courage is measured among Citizens. That is to say, he had never been afraid, though it was true that there had been very little occasion. But he was afraid now. He didn't want to be Translated.

The Wolf, Haendl, had put his finger on it: *Perhaps you still think Translation is a fulfillment.* Translation—the reward of Meditation, the gift bestowed on only a handful of gloriously transfigured persons. That was one thing. But the sort of Translation that was now involved was nothing like that—not if it happened to children; not if it happened to Gala Tropile; not if it happened to a machine.

And Glenn Tropile was involved in it.

Germyn turned restlessly.

If people who knew Glenn Tropile were likely to be Translated, and people who Meditated on Connectivity were likely to be Translated, then people who knew Glenn Tropile and didn't want to be Translated had better not Meditate on Connectivity.

It was very difficult to *not* think of Connectivity.

Endlessly he calculated sums in arithmetic in his mind, recited the Five Regulations, composed Greeting Poems and Verses on Viewing. And endlessly he kept coming back to Tropile, to Translation, to Connectivity. He didn't *want* to be Translated. But still the thought had a certain lure. What was it like? Did it hurt?

Well, probably not, he speculated. It was very fast, according to Haendl's report—if you could believe what an admitted Son of the Wolf reported. But Germyn had to.

Well, if it was fast—at that kind of speed, he thought, perhaps you would die instantly. Maybe Tropile was dead. Was that possible? No, it didn't seem so; after all, there was the fact of the connection between Tropile and so many of the recently Translated. What was the connection there? Or, generalizing, what connections were involved in—

He rescued himself from the dread word and summoned up the first image that came to mind. It happened to be Tropile's wife—Gala Tropile, who had disappeared herself, in this very room.

Gala Tropile. He stuck close to the thought of her, a little pleased with himself. That was the trick of *not* thinking of Connectivity—to think so hard and fully of something else as to leave no room in the mind for the unwanted thought. He pictured every line of her face, every wave of her stringy hair....

It was very easy that way. He was pleased.

CHAPTER XII

On Mount Everest, the sullen stream of off-and-on responses that was "mind" to the Pyramid had taken note of a new input signal.

It was not a critical mind. Its only curiosity was a restless urge to shove-and-haul, and there was no shove-and-haul about what to it was perhaps the analogue of a man's hunger pang. The input signal said: *Do thus.* It obeyed.

Call it craving for a new flavor. Where once it had patiently waited for the state that Citizens knew as Meditation on Connectivity, and the Pyramid itself perhaps knew as a stage of ripeness in the fruits of its wrist-watch mine, now it wanted a different taste. Unripe? Overripe? At any rate, different.

Accordingly, the high-frequency wheep, wheep changed in tempo and in key, and the bouncing echoes changed and...there was a ripe one to be plucked. (Its name was Innison.) And there another. (Gala Tropile.) And another, another—oh, many others—a babe from Tropile's nursery school and the Wheeling jailer and a woman Tropile once had coveted on the street.

Once the ruddy starch-to-sugar mark of ripeness had been what human beings called Meditation on Connectivity and the Pyramids knew as a convenient blankness. Now the sign was a sort of empathy with the Component named Tropile. It didn't matter to the Pyramid on Mount Everest. It swung its electrostatic scythe and the—call them Tropiletropes—were harvested.

It did not occur to the Pyramid on Mount Everest that a Component might be directing its actions. How could it?

Perhaps the Pyramid on Mount Everest wondered, if it knew how to wonder, when it noticed that different criteria were involved in selecting components these days. If it knew how to "notice." Surely even a Pyramid might wonder when, without warning or explanation, its orders were changed—not merely to harvest a different sort of Component, but to drag along with the flesh-and-blood needful parts a clanking assortment of machinery and metal, as began to happen. Machines? Why would the Pyramids need to Translate machines?

But why, on the other hand, would a Pyramid bother to question a directive, even if it were able to?

In any case, it didn't. It swung its scythe and gathered in what it was caused to gather in.

Men sometimes eat green fruit and come to regret it. Was it the same with Pyramids?

* * * *

And Citizen Germyn fell into the unsuspected trap. Avoiding Connectivity, he thought of Glenn Tropile—and the unfelt h-f pulses found him out.

He didn't see the Eye that formed above him. He didn't feel the gathering of forces that formed his trap. He didn't know that he was seized, charged, catapulted through space, caught, halted and drained. It happened too fast.

One moment he was in his bed; the next moment he was—elsewhere. There wasn't anything in between.

It had happened to hundreds of thousands of Components before him, but, for Citizen Germyn, what happened was in some ways different. He was not embalmed in nutrient fluid, formed and programmed to take his part in the Pyramid-structure, for he had not been selected by the Pyramid but by that single wild Component, Tropile. He arrived conscious, awake and able to move.

He stood up in a red-lit chamber. Vast thundering crashes of metal buffeted his ears. Heat sprang little founts of perspiration on his skin.

It was too much, too much to take in at once. Oily-skinned madmen, naked, were capering and shouting at him. It took him a moment to realize that they were not devils; this was not Hell; he was not dead.

"This way!" they were bawling at him. "Come on, hurry it up!"

He reeled, following their directions, across an unpleasantly warm floor, staggering and falling—the binary planet was a quarter denser than Earth—until he got his balance.

The capering madmen led him through a door—or sphincter or trap; it was not like anything he had ever seen. But it was a portal of a sort, and on the other side of it was something closer to sanity. It was another room, and though the light was still red, it was a paler, calmer red and the thundering ironmongery was a wall away. The madmen were naked, yes, but they were not mad. The oil on their skins was only the sheen of sweat.

"Where—where am I?" he gasped.

Two voices, perhaps three or four, were all talking at once. He could make no sense of it. Citizen Germyn looked about him. He was in a sort of chamber that formed a part of a machine that existed for the unknown purposes of the Pyramids on the binary planet. And he was alive—and not even alone.

He had crossed more than a million miles of space without feeling a thing. But when what the naked men were saying began to penetrate, the walls lurched around him.

It was true; he had been Translated.

right
WOLFBANE | 75

He looked dazedly down at his own bare body, and around at the room, and then he realized they were still talking: "—when you get your bearings. Feel all right now? Come on, Citizen, snap out of it!"

Germyn blinked.

Another voice said peevishly: "Tropile's got to find some other place to bring them in. That foundry isn't meant for human beings. Look at the shape this one is in! Some time somebody's going to come in and we won't spot him in time and—pfut!"

The first voice said: "Can't be helped. Hey! Are you all right?"

Citizen Germyn looked at the naked man in front of him and took a deep breath of hot, sour air. "Of course I'm all right," he said.

The naked man was Haendl.

* * * *

The Tropile-petal "said" to the Alla Narova-petal: "Got another one! It's Citizen Germyn!" The petal fluttered feebly in soundless laughter.

The Alla Narova-petal "said": "Glenn, come back! The whole propulsion-pneuma just went out of circuit!"

Tropile pulled his attention away from his human acquisitions in the chamber off the foundry and allowed himself to fuse with the woman-personality. Together they reached out and explored along the pathways they had laboriously traced. The propulsion-pneuma was the complex of navigation-computers, drive generators, course-vectoring units that their own unit had been originally part of—until Glenn Tropile, by waking its Components, had managed to divert it for purposes of his own. The two of them reached out into it—

Dead end.

It was out of circuit, as Alla Narova had said. One whole limb of their body—their new, jointly tenanted body, that spanned a whole planet and reached across space to Earth—had been lopped off. Quick, quick, they separated, traced separate paths. They came together again: Still dead end.

The dyad that was Tropile and the woman reached out to touch the others in the snowflake and communicated—not in words, not in anything as slow and as opaque as words: *The Pyramids have lopped off another circuit.* The compound personality of the snowflake considered its course of action, reached its decision, acted. Quick, quick, three of the other members of the snowflake darted out of the collective unit and went about isolating and tracing the exact area that had been affected.

Tropile: "We expected this. They couldn't help noticing sooner or later that something was going wrong."

Alla Narova: "But, Glenn, suppose they cut *us* out of circuit? We're stuck here. We can't move. We can't get out of the tanks. If they know that we are the source of their trouble—"

Tropile: "Let them know! That's what we've got the others here for!" He was cocky now, self-assured, fighting. For the first time in his life, he was free to fight—to let his Wolf blood strive to the utmost—and he knew what he was fighting for. This wasn't a matter of Haendl's pitiful tanks and carbines against the invulnerable Pyramids; this was the invulnerability of the whole Pyramid system turned against the Pyramids!

It was a warning, the fact that the Pyramids had become alert to danger, had begun cutting sections of their planetary communications system out of the main circuit. But as a warning, it didn't frighten Tropile; it only spurred him to action.

Quick, quick, he and the woman-personality dissolved, sped away. Figuratively they sought out the most restive Components they could find, shook them by the shoulder, tried to wake them. Actually—well, what is "actually?" The physical fact was surely that they didn't move at all, for they were bound to their tank and to the surgical joinings, each to each, at their temples. No crawling child in a playpen was more helplessly confined than Tropile and Alla Narova and the others.

And yet no human being had ever been more free.

* * * *

Regard that imbecile servant of Everyman, the thermostat.

He runs the furnace in Everyman's house, he measures the doneness of Everyman's breakfast toast, he valves the cooling fluid through the radiator of Everyman's car. If Everyman's house stays too hot or too cold, the man swears at the lackwit switch and maybe buys a new one to plug in. But he never, never thinks that his thermostat might be plotting against him.

Thermostat : Man = Man : Pyramid. Only that and nothing more. It was not in the nature of a Pyramid to think that its Components, once installed, could reprogram themselves. No Component ever had. (But before Glenn Tropile, no Component had been Wolf.)

When Tropile found himself, he found others. They were men and women, real persons with gonads and dreams. They had been caught at the moment of blankness—yes; and frozen into that shape, true. But they were palimpsest personalities on which the Pyramids had programmed their duties. Underneath the Pyramids' cabalistic scrawl, the men and women still remained. They had only to be reached.

Tropile and Alla Narova reached them—one at a time, then by scores. The Pyramids made that possible. The network of communication that they had created for their own purposes encompassed every cell of the race and all its works. Tropile reached out from his floating snowflake and went where he wished—anywhere within the binary planet; to the brooding Pyramid on Earth; through the Eyes, wherever he chose on Earth's surface.

Physically, he was scarcely able to move a muscle. But, oh, the soaring range of his mind and vision!

* * * *

Citizen Germyn was past shock, but just the same it was uncomfortable to be in a room with several dozen other persons, all of them naked. Uncomfortable. Once it would have been brain-shattering. For a Citizen to see his own Citizeness unclothed was gross lechery. To be part of a mixed and bare-skinned group was unthinkable. Or had been. Now it only made him uneasy.

He said numbly to Haendl: "Citizen, I pray you tell me what sort of place this is."

"Later," said Haendl gruffly, and led him out of the way. "Stay put," he advised. "We're busy."

And that was true. Something was going on, but Citizen Germyn couldn't make out exactly what it was. The naked people were worrying out a distribution of some sort of supplies. There were tools and there were also what looked to Citizen Germyn's unsophisticated eyes very much like guns. Guns? It was foolishness to think they were guns, Citizen Germyn told himself strongly. *Nobody* had guns. He touched the floor with an exploratory hand. It was warm and it shook with a nameless distant vibration. He shuddered.

Haendl came back; yes, they were guns. Haendl was carrying one.

"Ours!" he crowed. "That Tropile must've looted our armory at Princeton. By the looks of what's here, I doubt if he left a single round of ammunition. What the hell, they're more use here!"

"But what are we going to do with *guns*?"

Haendl looked at him with savage amusement. "Shoot."

Citizen Germyn said: "Please, Citizen. Tell me what this is all about."

Haendl sat down next to him on the warm, quivering floor and began fitting cartridges into a clip.

"We're fighting," he explained gleefully. "Tropile did it all. You've been shanghaied and so have all the rest of us. Tropile's alive! He's part of the Pyramid communications network—don't ask me how. But he's there and he has been hauling men and weapons and God knows what all up from Earth—you're on the binary planet now, you know—and we're going to bust things up so the Pyramids will *never* be able to put them back together again. Understand? Well, it doesn't matter if you don't. All you have to understand is that when I tell you to shoot this gun, you shoot."

Numbly, Citizen Germyn took the unfamiliar stock and barrel into his hands. Muscles he had forgotten he owned straightened the limp curve of his back, squared his shoulders and thrust out his chest.

It had been many generations since any of Citizen Germyn's people had known the feeling of being an Armed Man.

A naked woman with wild hair and a full, soft figure came toward them, jiggling in a way that agonized Citizen Germyn. He dropped his eyes to his gun and kept them there.

She cried: "Orders from Tropile! We've got to form a party and blow something up."

Haendl demanded: "Such as what?"

"I don't know what. I only know where. We've got a guide. And Tropile particularly asked for you, Haendl. He said you'd enjoy it."

And enjoy it Haendl did—anticipation was all over his face.

* * * *

They formed a party of a dozen. They armed themselves with the guns Tropile had levitated from the bulging warehouse at Princeton. They supplied themselves with gray metal cans of something that Haendl said were explosives, and with fuses and detonators to match, and they set off—with their guide.

A guide! It was a shambling, fearsome monster!

When Citizen Germyn saw it, he had to fight an almost irresistible temptation to be ill. Even the bare skins about him no longer mattered; this new horror canceled them out.

"What—What—" he strangled, pointing.

Haendl laughed raucously. "That's Joey."

"What's Joey?"

"He works for us," said Haendl, grinning.

Joey was neither human nor beast; it was not Pyramid; it was nothing Citizen Germyn had ever seen or imagined before. It crouched on many-jointed limbs, and even so was twice the height of a man. Its ropy arms and legs were covered with fine chitinous spines, laid on as close as hairs in a pelt, and sharp as thorns. There was a layer of chitin around its reddish eyes. What was more horrible than all, it spoke.

It said squeakily: "You all ready? Come on, snap it up! The Pyramids have got something big building up and we've got to squash it."

Citizen Germyn whispered feverishly to Haendl: "That voice! It sounds odd, yes—but isn't it Tropile's voice?"

"Sure it is! That's what old Joey is good for," said Haendl. "Tropile says he's telepathic, whatever that is. Makes it handy for us."

And it did. Telepathy was the alien's very special use to Glenn Tropile, for what Joey was in fact was another Component, from a previous wrist-watch mine. Joey's planet had once circled a star never visible from Earth; his home air was thin and his home sunlight was weak, and in consequence his race had developed a species of telepathy for communicating at long range. This was handy for the Pyramids, because it simplified the wiring. And it was equally handy for Glenn Tropile, once he managed to wake the creature—with its permission, he could use its body as a sort of walkie-talkie in directing the tactics of his shanghaied army.

That permission was very readily given. Joey remembered what the Pyramids had done to its own planet.

"Come on!" ordered Joey in Tropile's filtered voice, and they hastened through a straight and achingly cramped tunnel in single file, toward what Tropile had said was their target.

They had nearly reached it when, abruptly, there was a thundering of explosions ahead.

The party stopped, looked at each other, and got ready to move on more slowly.

At last it had started. The Pyramids were beginning to fight back.

CHAPTER XIII

Citizeness Roget Germyn, widow, woke from sleep like a well-mannered cat on the narrow lower third of the bed that her training had taught her to occupy, though it had been some days since her husband's Translation had emptied the Citizen's two-thirds permanently.

Someone had tapped gently on her door.

"I am awake," she called, in a voice just sufficient to carry.

A quiet voice said: "Citizeness, there is exceptional opportunity to Appreciate this morning. Come see, if you will. And I ask forgiveness for waking you."

She recognized the voice; it was the wife of one of her neighbors. The Citizeness made the appropriate reply, combining forgiveness and gratitude.

She dressed rapidly, but with appropriate pauses for reflection and calm, and stepped out into the street.

It was not yet daylight. Overhead, great sheets of soundless lightnings flared.

Inside Citizeness Germyn long-unfelt emotions stirred. There was something that was very like terror, and something that was akin to love. This was a generation that had never seen the aurora, for the ricocheting electron beams that cause it could not span the increasing distance between the orphaned Earth and its primary, Old Sol, and the small rekindled suns the Pyramids made were far too puny.

Under the sleeting aurora, small knots of Citizens stood about the streets, their faces turned up to the sky and illuminated by the distant light. It was truly an exceptional opportunity to Appreciate and they were all making the most of it.

Conscientiously, Citizeness Germyn sought out another viewer with whom to exchange comments on the spectacle above. "It is more bright than meteors," she said judiciously, "and lovelier than the freshly kindled Sun."

"Sure," said the woman. Citizeness Germyn, jolted, looked more closely. It was the Tropile woman—Gala? Was that her name? And what sort of name was *that*? But it fitted her well; she was the one who had been wife to Wolf and, more likely than not, part Wolf herself.

Still, the case was not proved. Citizeness Germyn said honestly: "I have never seen a sight to compare with this in all my life."

Gala Tropile said indifferently: "Yeah. Funny things are happening all the time these days, have you noticed? Ever since Glenn turned out to be—" She stopped.

Citizeness Germyn rapidly diagnosed her embarrassment and acted to cover it up. "That is so. I have seen Eyes a hundred times and yet has there been a Translation with the Eyes? No. But there have been Translations. It is queer."

"I suppose so," Gala Tropile said, looking upward at the display. She sighed.

Over their heads, a formed Eye was drifting slowly about, but neither of the women noticed it. The shifting lights in the sky obscured it.

"I wonder what causes that stuff," Gala Tropile said idly.

Citizeness Germyn made no attempt to answer. It was not the sort of question that would normally have occurred to her and therefore not a sort to which she could reply.

Moreover, it was not the question closest to Gala Tropile's heart at that moment—nor, for that matter, the question closest to Citizeness Germyn's. The question that underlay the thoughts of both was: *I wonder what happened to my husband.*

It was strange, but true, that the answers to all their questions were very nearly the same.

* * * *

The Alla-Narova mind said sharply: "Glenn, come back!"

Tropile withdrew from scanning the distant dark street. He laughed soundlessly. "I was watching my wife. God, we're giving them fits down there! The Pyramids must be churning things up, too—the sky is full of auroral displays. Looks like there's plenty of h-f bouncing around the atmosphere."

"Pay attention!" the Alla-Narova mind commanded.

"All right." Obediently, Tropile returned to the war he was waging.

It was a strange conflict, strangely fought. Tropile's mind searched the abysses and tunnels of the Pyramid planet, and what he sensed or saw was immediately communicated to all of the awakened Components who were his allies.

It was a godlike position. Was he sane? There was no knowing. Sanity no longer meant anything to Tropile. He was beyond such human affairs as lunacy or its reverse. An insane man is one who is out of joint with his environment. Tropile was himself his environment. His mind encompassed two planets and the space between. He saw with a thousand eyes. He worked with a thousand hands.

And he struck mighty blows.

The weakness of a network that reaches everywhere is that it is everywhere vulnerable. If a teletype repeater in Omaha garbles a single digit, printing units in Atlanta and Bangor will type out errors. Tropile, by striking at the Pyramids' net at a thousand points, garbled their communications and made them nearly useless. More, he took the Pyramid network for his own. The Tropile-pulse sped through the neurone guides of the Pyramid net, and what it encountered it mastered, and what it mastered it changed.

The Pyramids discovered that they had been attacked.

Frantically (if they felt frenzy), the Pyramids replaced Components; the Tropile-pulse woke the new ones. Unbelievingly (did they know how to "believe"?), the Pyramids isolated contaminated circuits; the Tropile-pulse bypassed them.

Desperately (or joyously or uffishly—one term fits exactly as well as another), the Pyramids returned to shove-and-haul, and there was much destruction, and some Components died.

But by then, the Components had reprogrammed themselves.

* * * *

The first job had been the matter of finding hands for the Tropile-brain to work with. Bring hands in, then! Tropile commanded the Pyramids' network and obediently it was done. The Translation mechanism, the electrostatic scythe that had harvested so many crops from the wristwatch mines, suffered a change and went to work not for the pickers but for the fruit.

The essential change in the operation of that particular pneuma had been simple; first, to "harvest" or "Translate" the men and women Tropile wanted as fighters instead of the meditative Citizen kind. Second, to divert the new arrivals to where they would not go straight to deep-freeze. It happened that the only alternate space Tropile could find was a sort of foundry that was nearly Hell, but that was only a detail. The important thing was that new helpers were arriving, with minds of their own and the capacity to move and act.

Then Tropile needed to communicate with them. He found the alien, ropy-limbed Component whose name vaguely approached "Joey." Joey's limited sense of telepathy was needed and so, with enormous difficulty, Tropile and Alla Narova, combined, managed to reach and wake it.

And so he had an army, captured humans for troops, an awakened Joey for liaison.

Tropile was lord of two worlds. Not only the Pyramids were under his thumb, but his own fellow humans whom he had drafted into his service. They ate when a captured circuit he controlled fed synthetic mush into troughs for them. They breathed because a captured circuit he directed created air. They would return to Earth when—and only when—a captured circuit he operated sent them home.

Sane?

By what standards?

And what difference did it make?

CHAPTER XIV

With a series of grinding shocks, like an enormous earthquake-fault relieving a strain, the Pyramids began to fight back.

"Tropile!" the Alla-Narova mind called urgently.

Tropile flashed to the trouble spot. Through eyes that were not his own, Tropile scanned the honeycombed world of the Pyramids. There was an area where huge and ancient vehicles lay covered with the slow dust of centuries, and the vehicles were beginning to move.

Caterpillar-treaded hauling machines were loading themselves with what Tropile judged were quickly synthesized explosives. Almost forgotten wheeled vehicles were creeping mindlessly out of nearly abandoned storage sections and lumbering painfully along the tunnels of the planet.

"Coming toward us," Tropile diagnosed dispassionately.

Alla Narova queried: "They mean to fight?"

"Of course. You see if you can penetrate the circuit that controls them. I—" already he was flashing away—"I'll get to the boys through Joey."

It was queer, looking through the eyes of the alien they called Joey; colors were all wrong, perspective was flat. But he could see, though cloudily. He saw Haendl joyously fitting a bayonet—*a bayonet!*—to a rifle; he saw Citizen Germyn, naked but square-shouldered, puffing valiantly along in the rear.

Tropile said through the strange vocal cords that belonged to the alien: "You'll have to hurry." (Strange to speak in words again!) "The Pyramids are heading toward the chambers where the Components are kept. I think they mean to kill us."

He flashed away, located the area, flashed back. "You'll have to go without me—I mean without Joey-me. The only way I see to get there is through a narrow little ventilation tunnel—I guess ventilation is what it was for."

Quickly (but against the familiar race of thought, it seemed agonizingly slow) he laid out the route for them and left; it was up to them. Watching from a dozen viewpoints at once, he saw the slow creep of the Pyramids' machines and the slower intersecting march of his little army. He studied the alternate cross routes and contrived to block some of them by interfering with the control-circuits of the emergency doors and portals.

But there were some circuits he could not control. The Pyramids had withdrawn whole sections of their net and areas of the planet were now hidden from him entirely. Sections of the vast maintenance-propulsion-manufacturing complex were no longer subject to his interference or control.

* * * *

It would be, Tropile thought dispassionately, a rather close thing. The chances were perhaps six out of ten that his hastily assembled task force would be able to intercept the convoy of automatic machines before it could reach the racks of nutrient tanks.

And if they were not in time?

Tropile almost laughed out loud, if that had been possible. Why, then, his body would be destroyed! How trivial a thing to worry about! He began to forget he owned a body; surely it was someone else's bone and tissue that lay floating in the eight-branched snowflake. He knew that this was not so. He knew that if his body were killed, he would die. And yet there was no sense of fear, no personal involvement. It was an interesting problem in scheduling and nothing more.

Would the human fighters get there in time?

Perhaps the automatic machines had senses, for as the first of the humans burst into the tunnel they were using, a few hundred yards ahead of the lead load-carrier, the machines shuddered to a stop. Pause for a second; then, laboriously, they began to back toward the nearest of the side passages that Tropile had been unable to block. He scanned it hurriedly. Good, good! The circuits surrounding the passage proper were out of his reach, but it led to another passage, an abandoned pipeline of sorts, it seemed to be. And *that* he could reach....

Patiently (how slowly the machines crept along!) he waited until one of the Pyramids' machines bearing explosives passed through an enormous valve in the line—and then the valve was thrown.

The explosion triggered every vehicle in the line. The damage was complete.

Scratch one threat from the Pyramids—

And almost at once, there was another urgent call from Alia Narova: "Tropile, quickly!"

* * * *

The Pyramids were the mightiest race of warriors the Universe had ever known. They were invulnerable and unconquerable, except from within. Like Alexander the Great, they had met every enemy and whipped them all. And, like dying Alexander, they writhed and raged against the tiny, unseen bacillus within themselves.

Blindly, almost suicidally, the Pyramids returned to their ancient principle of shove-and-haul.

The geography of the binary planet was like a hive of bees, nearly featureless on the surface, but internally a congeries of tunnels, chambers, warrens, rooms, tubes and amphitheaters. Machinery and metal Components were everywhere thick under the planet's crust. The more delicate and more useful Components of flesh and blood were, to a degree, concentrated in a few areas....

And one of those areas had disappeared.

Tropile, battering futilely with his mind at the periphery of the vanished area, cried sharply to Alla Narova and the others: "It looks as though they've broken a piece right out of the planet! Everything stops here—there's a physical gap which I can't cross. Hurry, one of you—what was this section for?"

"Propulsion."

"I see." Tropile hesitated, confused for the first time since his awakening. "Wait."

He retreated to the snowflake and communed with the other eight-branched members, now become something that resembled his general staff. He told them—most of them already knew, but the telling took so little time that it was simpler to go through it from beginning to end:

"The Pyramids attempted to cut the propulsion-pneuma out of circuit some seconds or days ago and were unsuccessful; we awakened additional Components and were able to maintain contact with it. They have now apparently cut it loose from the planet itself. I do not think it is far, but there is a physical space between."

"The importance of the propulsion-pneuma is this: It controls the master generators of electrostatic force, which are used both to move this planet and ours, and to perform the act of Translation. If the Pyramids control it, they may be able to take us out of circuit, perhaps back to Earth, perhaps throwing us into space, where we will die. The question for decision: How can we counteract this move?"

* * * *

A rush of voices all spoke at once; it was no trick for Tropile and the others to sort them out and follow the arguments of each, but it cannot be reproduced.

At last, one said: "There is a way. I will do it."

It was Alla Narova.

"What is the way?" Tropile demanded, curiously alarmed.

"I shall go with them, trace the areas the Pyramids are attempting to isolate, place my entire self—" by this she meant her "concentration," her "psyche," that part of all of them which flashed along the neurone guides unhampered by flesh or distance—"in the most likely point they will next cut loose. And then I shall cause the propulsion units on the severed sections to force them back into circuit."

Tropile objected: "But you don't know what will happen! We have never been cut off from our physical bodies, Alla Narova. It may be death. It may not be possible at all. You don't know!"

Alla Narova thought a smile and a farewell. She said: "No, I do not." And then, "Good-by, Tropile."

She had gone.

Furiously, Tropile hurled himself after her, but she was quick as he, too quick to catch; she was gone. *Foolishness, foolishness!* he shouted silently. How could she do an insane, chancy thing like this?

And yet what else was there to do? They were all ignorant babes, temporarily successful because there had been no defense against them, for who expects babes to rise up in rebellion? They didn't *know*. For all they could guess or imagine, the Pyramids had an effective counter for any move they might make. Temporary success meant nothing. It was the final decision that counted, when either the Pyramids were vanquished or the men, and what steps were needed to make that decision favor the men were anyone's guess—Alla Narova's was as good as his.

Tropile could only watch and wait.

Through a great many viewpoints and observers, he was able to see roughly what happened.

* * * *

There was a section of the planet next the severed chunk where the mind and senses of Alla Narova lay coiled for a moment—and were gone. For what it had accomplished, her purpose succeeded. She had been taken. She was out of circuit.

The overwhelming consciousness of loss that flooded through Glenn Tropile was something outside of all his experience.

Next to him in the snowflake, the body which he had learned to think of as the body of Alla Narova twisted sharply as though waking from a dream—and lay flaccid, floating in the fluid.

"Alla Narova! *Alla Narova!*"

There was no answer.

A voice came piercingly: "Tropile! Here now, quickly!"

Good-by, Alla Narova! He flashed away to see what the other voice had found. Great mindless boulders were chipping away from the crust of the binary planet and whirling like midges in the void around it.

"What is it?" cried one of the others.

Tropile had no answer. It was the Pyramids, clearly. Were they attempting to demolish their own planet? Were they digging away at the crust to uncover the maggot's-nest of awakened Components beneath?

"The air!" cried Tropile sharply, and knew it was true. What the Pyramids were up to was a simple delousing operation. If you could destroy their own machinery for maintaining air and pressure and temperature, they would destroy all living things within—including Haendl and Citizen Germyn and thus, in the final analysis, including the bodies of Tropile and his awakened fellows. For without the mobile troops to defend their helpless cocoons against the machines of the Pyramids, the limp bodies could be destroyed as easily as a larva under a farmer's heel.

So Alla Narova had failed.

Alone against the Pyramids, she had been unable to bring the recaptured sections back into the circuit that Tropile's Components now dominated. It was the end of hope; but it was not the fear of defeat and damnation for the Earth that paralyzed Tropile. It was Alla Narova, gone from him forever.

The Pyramids were too strong.

And yet, he thought, quickening, they had been too strong before and still a weak spot had been found!

"Think," he ordered himself desperately.

And then again: "Think!" Components stirred restlessly around him, questioning. "Think!" he cried mightily. "All of you, think! Think of your lives and hopes!

"Think!

"Hope!

"Worry!

"Dream!"

The Components were reaching toward him now, wonderingly. He commanded them violently: "Do it—concentrate, wish, think! Let your minds run free and think of Earth, pleasant grass and warm sun! Think of loving and sweat and heartbreak! Think of death and birth! *Think*, for the love of heaven, *think*!"

And the answer was not in sound, but it was deafening.

* * * *

In the cut-off sections, Alla Narova's soaring mind lay trapped. It had not been enough; she could not force her will against the dull inflexibility of the Pyramids....

Until that inflexible will began to waver.

There was a leakage of thought.

It maddened and baffled the Pyramids. The whole neuronic network was resounding to a babble of thoughts and emotions that, to a Pyramid, were utterly demented! The rousing Component minds throbbed with urge and emotion that were new to Pyramid experience. What could a Pyramid make of a human's sex drive? Or of the ropy-armed aliens' passionate deification of the Egg? What of hunger and thirst and the blazing Wolf-need for odds and advantage that streamed out of such as Tropile?

They wavered, unsure. Their reactions were slow and very confused.

For Alla Narova succeeded in her purpose. She was able to reach out across the space and barrier to Tropile and the propulsion-pneuma was back in circuit. The section that controlled the master generators of the electronic scythe lay under his hands.

"Now!" he cried, and all of the Components reached out to grasp and move.

"Now!" And the central control was theirs; the full flood of power from the generators was at their command.

"Now! Now! Now!" And they reached out, with a fat pencil of electrostatic force and caught the sluggish, brooding Pyramid on Mount Everest.

It had squatted there without motion for more than two centuries. Now it quivered and seemed to draw back, but the probing pencil caught it, and whirled it, and hurled it up and out of Earth, into the tiny artificial sun.

It struck with a flare of blue-white light.

"One gone!" gloated Tropile. "Alla Narova, are you there?"

"Still here," she called from a great distance. "Again?"

"Again!"

They reached for the Pyramids and found them, wherever they were. Some lay close to the surface of the binary planet, and some were hundreds of miles within, and a few, more desperate than the others or merely assigned to the task, they discovered at the very portal of the single spaceship of the Pyramids.

But wherever they were and whatever they chose to do, each one of them was found and seized. They came wriggling and shaking, like trout on an angler's line. They came bursting through layer on layer of impenetrable metal that, nevertheless, they penetrated. They came by the dozens and scores, and at last by the thousands; but they came.

There were more and more flares of blue-white light on the tiny sun—so many that Tropile found himself scouring the planet in a desperate search for one surviving Pyramid—not to destroy as an enemy, but to keep for a specimen.

But he searched in vain.

The Pyramids were·destroyed, gone. There was not one left. The Earth lay open and free under its tiny sun for the first time in centuries.

It had been a strange war, but a short one.

And it was over.

CHAPTER XIV

Tropile swam up out of hammering blackness into daylight and pain.

It *hurt*. He was being born again—coming back to life—and it had all the agonies of parturition, except that they were visited upon the creature being born, himself. There were crushing blows at his temples that pounded and pained like no other ache he had ever felt. He moaned raspingly.

Someone moved blurrily over his shut eyes. He felt something sting sharply at the base of his brain. Then it tingled, warming his scalp, comforting it, numbing it. Pain went slowly away.

He opened his eyes.

Four masked torturers were leaning over him. He stared, not understanding; but the eyes were not torturers' eyes, and in a moment the masks came off. Surgical masks—and the faces beneath the masks were human faces.

Surgeons and nurses.

He blinked at them and said groggily: "Where am we?" And then he remembered.

He was back on Earth; he was merely human again.

Someone came bustling into the room and he knew without looking that it was Haendl.

"We beat them, Tropile!" Haendl cried. "No, cancel that. *You* beat them. We've destroyed every Pyramid there was, and a nice hot fire they're making up there on the sun, eh? Beautiful work, Tropile. Beautiful! You're a credit to the name of Wolf!"

The surgeons stirred uneasily, but apparently, Tropile thought, there had been changes, for they did no more than that.

Tropile touched his temples fretfully and his fingers rested on gauze bandages. It was true: he was out of circuit. The long reach of his awareness was cut short at his skull; there was no more of the infinite sweep and grasp he had known as part of the snowflake in the nutrient fluid.

"Too bad," he whispered hopelessly.

"What?" Haendl frowned. The nurse next to him whispered something and he nodded. "Oh, I see. You're still a little groggy, right? Well, that's not hard to understand—they tell me it was a tricky job of surgery, separating you from that gunk the Pyramids had wired into your head."

"Yes," said Tropile, and closed his ears, though Haendl went on talking. After a while, Tropile pushed himself up and swung his legs over the side of the operating table. He was naked. Once that would have bothered him enormously, but now it didn't seem to matter.

"Find me some clothes, will you?" he asked. "I'm back. I might as well start getting used to it."

* * * *

Glenn Tropile found that he was a returning hero, attracting a curious sort of hero-worship wherever he went. It was not, he thought after careful analysis, *exactly* what he might have expected. For instance, a man who went out and killed a dragon in the old days was received with great gratitude and rejoicing, and if there was a prince's daughter around, he married her. Fair enough, after all. And Tropile had slain a foe more potent than any number of dragons.

But he tested the attention he received and found no gratitude in it. It was odd.

What it was like most of all, he thought, was the sort of attention a reigning baseball champion might get—in a country where cricket was the national game. He had done something which, everybody agreed, was an astonishing feat, but about which nobody seemed to care. Indeed, there was an area of accusation in some of the attention he got.

Item: nearly ninety thousand erstwhile Components had now been brought back to ambient life, most of them with their families long dead, all of them a certain drain on the limited resources of the planet. And what was Glenn Tropile going to do about it?

Item: the old distinctions between Citizen and Wolf no longer made much sense now that so many Componentized Citizens had fought shoulder to shoulder with Componentized Sons of the Wolf. But didn't Glenn Tropile think he had gone a little too far *there*?

And item—looking pretty far ahead, of course, but still—well, just what *was* Glenn Tropile going to do about providing a new sun for Earth, when the old one wore out and there would be no Pyramids to tend the fire?

He sought refuge with someone who would understand him. That, he was pleased to realize, was easy. He had come to know several persons extremely well. Loneliness, the tortured loneliness of his youth, was permanently behind him, *definitely*.

For example, he could seek out Haendl, who would understand everything very well.

Haendl said: "It is a bit of a letdown, I suppose. Well, hell with it; that's life." He laughed grimly. "Now that we've got rid of the Pyramids, there's plenty of other work to be done. Man, we can breathe now! We can plan ahead! This planet has maundered along in its stupid, rutted, bogged-down course too many years already, eh? It's time we took over! And we'll be doing it, I promise you. You know, Tropile—" he sniggered—"I only regret one thing."

"What's that?" Tropile asked cautiously.

"All those weapons, out of reach! Oh, I'm not *blaming* you. But you can see what a lot of trouble it's going to be now, stocking up all over again—and there isn't much we can do about bringing order to this tired old world, is there, until we've got the guns to do it with again?"

Tropile left him much sooner than he had planned.

* * * *

Citizen Germyn, then? The man had fought well, if nothing else. Tropile went to find him and, for a moment at least, it was very good. Germyn said: "I've been doing a lot of thinking, Tropile. I'm glad you're here." He sent his wife for refreshments, and decorously she brought them in, waited for exactly one minute, and then absented herself.

Tropile burst into speech as soon as she left. "I'm beginning to realize what has happened to the human race, Germyn. I don't mean just now, when we licked the Pyramids and so on. No, I mean hundreds of years ago, what happened when the Pyramids arrived, and what has been happening since. Did you ever hear of Indians, Germyn?"

Germyn frowned minutely and shrugged.

"They were, oh, hundreds *and* hundreds of years ago. They were a different color and not very civilized—of course, nobody was then. But the Indians were nomads, herdsmen, hunters—like that. And the white people came from Europe and wanted this country for themselves. So they took it. And do you know something? I don't think the Indians ever knew what hit them."

"*They* didn't know about land grants and claiming territory for the crown and church missions and expanding populations. They didn't have those things. It's true that they learned pretty well, by and by—at least they learned things like guns and horses and firewater; they didn't have those things, either, but they could see some sense to them, you know. But I really don't think the Indians ever knew exactly what the Europeans were up to, until it was too late to matter.

"And it was the same with us and the Pyramids, only more so. What the devil *did* they want? I mean, yes, we found out what they did with the Translated people. But what were they *up* to? What did they *think*? *Did* they think? You know, I've got a kind of a crazy idea—maybe it's not crazy, maybe it's the truth. Anyway, I've been thinking. Suppose even the *Pyramids* weren't the Pyramids? We never talked to one of them. We never gave it a Rorschach or tested its knee jerks. We licked them, but we don't know anything about them. We don't even know if they were the guys that started the whole bloody thing, or if they were just sort of super-sized Components themselves. Do we?

"And meanwhile, here's the human race, up against something that it not only can't understand, same as the Indians couldn't the whites, but that it can't begin to make a *guess* about. At least the Indians had a clue now and then, you know—I mean they'd see the sailors off the great white devil ship making a beeline for the Indian women and so on, and they'd begin to understand there was *something* in common. But we didn't have that much.

"So what did we do? Why, we did like the reservation Indians. We turned inward. We got loaded on firewater—Meditation—and we closed our minds to the possibility of ever expanding again. And there we were, all tied up in our own knots. Most of the race rebelled against action, because it had proven useless—Citizens. A few of the race rebelled against *that*, because it was not only useless but *deliberately* useless—Wolves. But they're the same kind of people. You've seen that for yourself, right? And—"

Tropile stopped, suddenly aware that Citizen Germyn was looking tepidly pained.

"What's the matter?" Tropile demanded harshly.

Citizen Germyn gave him the faint deprecatory Quirked Smile. "I know you thought you were a Wolf, but—I told you I've been thinking a lot, and that's what I was thinking about. *Truly*, Citizen, you do yourself no good by pretending that you really thought you were Wolf. Clearly you were not; the rest of us might have been fooled, but certainly you couldn't fool yourself.

"Now here's what I think you ought to do. When I found you were coming, I asked several rather well-known Citizens to come here later this evening. There won't be any embarrassment. I only want you to talk to them and set the record straight, so that this terrible blemish will no longer be held against you. Times change and perhaps a certain latitude is advisable now, but certainly you don't want—"

Tropile also left Citizen Germyn sooner than he had expected to.

* * * *

There remained Alla Narova, but, queerly, she was not to be found.

Instantly it became clear to Tropile that it was she above all whom he needed to talk to. He remembered the shared beauty of their plunging drive through the neurone-guides of the Pyramids, the linked and inextricable flow of their thoughts and of their most hidden feelings.

She could not be very far, he thought numbly, cursing the blindness of his human eyes, the narrowness of his human senses. Time was when two worlds could not have hidden her from him; but that time was gone. He walked from place to place with the angry resentful tread of one used to riding—no, to flying, or faster than flying. He asked after her. He searched.

And at last he found—not her. A note. At one of the stations where the re-awakened Components were funneled back into human affairs, there was a letter waiting for him:

> I'm sure you will look for me. Please don't. You thought that there were no secrets between us, but there was one.
>
> When I was Translated, I was sixty-one years old. Two years before that, I was caught in a collapsing building; my legs are useless, and I had grown quite fat. I do not want you to see me fat and old.
>
> Alla Narova.

And that was that, and at last Glenn Tropile turned to the last person of all those on his list who had known him well. Her name was Gala Tropile.

* * * *

She had got thinner, he observed. They sat together quietly and there was considerable awkwardness, but then he noticed that she was weeping. Comforting her ended the awkwardness and he found that he was talking:

"It was like being a god, Gala! I swear, there's no feeling like it. I mean it's like—well, maybe if you'd just had a baby, and invented fire, and moved a mountain, and transmuted lead into gold—maybe if you'd done all of those things, then you might have some idea. But I was everywhere at once, Gala, and I could do anything! I fought a whole world of Pyramids, do you realize that? Me! And now I come back to—"

He stopped her in time; it seemed she was about to weep again.

He went on: "No, Gala, don't misunderstand, I don't hold anything against you. You were right to leave me in the field. What did I have to offer you? Or myself, for that matter? And I don't know that I have anything now, but—"

He slammed his fist against the table. "They talk about putting the Earth back in its orbit! Why? And how? My God, Gala, we don't know *where* we are. Maybe we could tinker up the gadgets the Pyramids used and turn our course backward—but do you know what Old Sol looks like? I don't. I never saw it.

"And neither did you or anyone else alive.

"It was like being a god—

"And they talk about going back to things as they were—

"I'm sick of that kind of thinking! Wolves or Citizens, they're dead on their feet and don't know it. I suppose they'll snap out of it in time, but I can't wait. I won't live that long.

"Unless—"

He paused and looked at her, confused.

Gala Tropile met her husband's eyes.

"Unless what, Glenn?"

He shrugged and turned away.

"Unless you go back, you mean." He stared at her; she nodded. "You want to go back," she said, without stress. "You don't want to stay here with me, do you? You want to go back into that tub of soup again and float like a baby. You don't want to *have* babies—you want to *be* one."

"Gala, you don't understand. We can own the Universe. I mean mankind can. And I can do it. Why not? There's nothing for me—"

"That's right, Glenn. There's nothing for you here. Not any more."

He opened his mouth to speak, looked at her, spread his hands helplessly. He didn't look back as he walked out the door, but he knew that his back was turned not only on the woman who happened to be his wife, but on mankind and all of the flesh.

* * * *

It was night outside, and warm. Tropile stood in the old street surrounded by the low, battered houses—and he could make them new and grand! He looked up at the stars that swung in constellations too new and changeable to have names. *There* was the Universe.

Words were no good; there was no explaining things in words. Naturally he couldn't make Gala or anyone else understand, for flesh couldn't grasp the realities of mind and spirit that were liberated from flesh. Babies! A home! And the whole grubby animal business of eating and drinking and sleeping! How could anyone ask to stay in the mire when the stars challenged overhead?

He walked slowly down the street, alone in the night, an apprentice godling renouncing mortality. There was nothing here for him, so why this sense of loss?

Duty said (or was it Pride?): "Someone must give up the flesh to control Earth's orbit and weather—why not you?"

Flesh said (or was it his soul—whatever that was?): "But you will be *alone*."

He stopped, and for a moment he was poised between destiny and the dust....

Until he became aware of footsteps behind him, running, and Gala's voice: "Wait! Wait, Glenn! I want to go with you!"

And he turned and waited, but only until she caught up, and then he went on.

But not—forever and always again—not alone.